Mid-life
Crisis

Mid-life Crisis

a novel

T Jessop

The Book Guild Ltd

First published in Great Britain in 2017 by
The Book Guild Ltd
9 Priory Business Park
Wistow Road, Kibworth
Leicestershire, LE8 0RX
Freephone: 0800 999 2982
www.bookguild.co.uk
Email: info@bookguild.co.uk
Twitter: @bookguild

Typeset in Minion Pro

Printed and bound in Great Britain by 4edge Limited

ISBN 978 1912083 862

British Library Cataloguing in Publication Data.
A catalogue record for this book is available from the British Library.

It is what it is
I am who I am
You are who you are
Fubar
I love you all

Tuesday 27th December 2013

The day began after being woken by the ever-annoying sound of the alarm clock. Once showered and dressed I was sat at the kitchen table drinking my second cup of tea, pondering the events of last night, a dark mood hanging over me as the morning brought the realisation of losing my best friend: today is the day that Chloe and Paul left for Scotland to begin their new life.

She spent her last night here with me and the girls having a goodbye drink. I was pretty much holding it together until she proceeded to have a meltdown about whether or not they're doing the right thing. Fighting back the urge to scream 'Don't go! 'we all dutifully reminded her that Scotland is not the other side of the world, it's just a bit further to visit. With plenty of tears and equal amounts of snot we all reassured her that it'll change nothing about our friendship.

Chloe is a born and bred Walthamstow girl; what the hell is she doing moving away? Far far away, I might add. My best friend: damn, it seems like only yesterday when we were sat next to each other on our first day at infants' school, an unbreakable bond that carried us through to the juniors, then onto middle school, where we then formed the trio as Julie joined our clique. High school introduced us to Elizabeth who became the fourth musketeer; still never worked out how that happened.

Paul being best mates with my Joe, it seemed inevitable that Chloe and Paul ended up as a couple. We have all been bridesmaids at each other's weddings, stood endless hours at Maternity waiting for the arrival of each other's babies. Thick or thin, rain or shine… a pinky shake between two six-year-olds to be by the other's side till the end. Look at us all now: Elizabeth, married to Arthur, a successful lawyer and living in New York; Julie, a senior partner in a law firm; we own our own building company; and Paul is the most sought-after roofer within 50 miles. So who'd have thought they'd end up sheep farming, in bloody Scotland.

I'm not surprised she panicked last night: investing everything they have would shit anyone up; if it doesn't work, they're screwed. Julie repeated her offer that in the event of bankruptcy they can both go live with her, on the one condition that Paul has to sleep in Julie's bed, with her – hussy. This quickly served as a reminder as to why Chloe wanted to move so far away in the first place. At least Julie's consistent, she's been like that since we first met her; maybe we should all get away from Julie's slutty advances towards our husbands. I have no doubt Chloe and Paul will be fine. There was the same panic fit with Elizabeth when Arthur got promoted overseas to the New York office; she found it a wrench at first but settled in fine. We've all been friends for so long it's going to be weird not having her round the corner. I know I'm being silly. What's distance between great mates? xx

Having got sick of drinking tea and wallowing in self-pity I took a stroll down to the nightclub. Ah, Mickey's, where memories are made and hearts have been broken. I'd never noticed before that the outside of the building is blue. Entering the lobby in daylight was odd, and even weirder was to be one of only three people milling about inside. The silence was deafening; what a difference the bass and the metal detectors make in the evenings when it comes to life. Emblazoned on a poster: '80s Night 25th February 8.00pm'. Time once again to dust off the white boots and ra ra's, woo hoo! I purchased half a dozen tickets, thanked the girl in the kiosk and left.

80s + Chloe = lol. She'll be travelling back to the heather

hills with alcohol poisoning Elizabeth will probably fly in on the 24th and go straight to the hotel. I called Julie who said she has an appointment on that day to pick up her custom-made suits from Kensington, reckons she'll be home by 5pm, thus giving her plenty of time to get ready by eight. Yeah, right, the amount of slap that girl puts on must take a minimum of four hours. Meow… jealousy is a terrible thing. xx

Dinner done, washing up in the dishwasher, and I've finished putting the final touches to our beautiful daughter's birthday cake. Just called out to Joe to whip down the corner shop and get me some cigarettes, to which he responded, 'Get stuffed, it's as cold as a witch's tit out there.' I'll take that as a 'No', then. Looking out the window I'd say it's definitely going to snow again; that reminds me, must get some more dandruff shampoo for the dog. Envying Julie's sister right now as Penny, Mark and the kids have spent Christmas in Malta with his parents and are not coming back until the New Year.

Positives: Hair cut and Mickey's booked.
Negatives: Chloe has moved to the other side of the world.

Wednesday 28th December 2013

Haven't seen much of Leigh today, no sooner had she opened her presents she was *gone*. Daughters! Who'd have them? Unbelievably I was blown out for the company of her mates, pizza and some movie called *Divergent* with some geezer called Theo James, who is as 'fit as hell' - I wouldn't know, I weren't invited.

It's bothered me more than I'm letting on. Don't know what bit is worse, that I've been pushed aside or that my daughter is now seventeen. Shit, where have the years gone? Seems like only yesterday when we brought home the tiny bundle of pink, now she looks similar to my daughter but with less clothing and more make-up.

Having nothing better to do than sulk I rang Chloe. It seems she had a restless first night on the farm. Insomnia brought on by the lack of sirens and turfed out of the pub sing-songs. Apart from the tiredness she was in an excited mood and I didn't want to rain on her parade with my ever-growing foul mood; instead I told her I'd leave her in peace and would catch up in a few days. I put some washing on and phoned my mum, not wanting but needing to have a rant about Leigh's heartless rejection. Mum laughed and mumbled something about 'what goes around' followed by, 'If you think you feel a bit miffed now, wait till they leave home and you get empty nest syndrome'. Yeah, good talk, cheers, Mum. Don't know why I bothered. I'm now sitting in the conservatory watching yet more snow settling on the lawn and I just told the dog not to bother going out as it's freezing; it may look pretty but it's cold. *Christ* now I sound like a pensioner. Oh well, this won't do, I now have another cake to make as its Tony's birthday tomorrow, and unlike his sister I know my youngest won't let me down.

Positives:?
Negatives: Daughters.

Thursday 29th December 2013

It's only 5am and I've got serious cotton mouth, thanks to Julie, Chris, Abigail and Tina dropping by last night to bring Leigh and Tony's gifts round. We ended up consuming four bottles of wine which wasn't hard for me, feeling the way I did because of my lovely daughter. All faith lies on Tony this morning. I know my baby boy will make up for yesterday.

Kids are just bloody hateful. Not liking Leigh's desertion yesterday I was determined to share this day with Tony all was going well until five minutes ago when I noticed a note on the fridge: 'Open pressies when I get home, gone paintballing, don't worry about dinner, grab something out, Love you xxxxxx'. Er, hello! When did I get sacked? Am I not the person they most want to spend the day with, did I not give them life? Not liking this one sodding bit. Joe's getting on my wick with the, 'They're growing up, they don't wanna hang about with us, we're old.' Er, you may be, but not me, mate.

Hoping to walk off the banging headache, I popped into Chris's on the way back from town this afternoon. She opened the door wearing what looked like a forensic overall with a dust cover over her mouth and a wad of bog roll wedged up each nostril. If it had been anyone else but my sister I'd have been stunned. Molly and Baby had been throwing up all-night, hence the protective gear. The only protection needed is from Chris's cooking: the kids told me she was forcing them to try her new Indian dishes.

Chris said that Abigail took a sickie so at least I'm not the only one that's suffering after last night.

Positives: Not the only idiot with a hangover.
Negatives: Sons.
Feeling really sorry for myself. xx

Friday 30th December 2013

Been up since the crack of dawn. Again.
Feeling downright miserable. Again.

Accumulation of Chloe leaving, another year ending and the realisation that the kids no longer need me.

Abigail blew Chris out for lunch in favour of the hairdressers so Chris asked me if I wanted to go round Nan's with her. I passed on the offer: with Nan being ancient I'd expect her to waffle on about all her aches, pains and ailments, but there are not enough hours or indeed years left in my life to listen to Chris relay hers.

Chloe called to tell me she'd been chopping logs all day. Paul let her do this for three hours before telling her that they can buy them already split. She is not a happy bunny.

At least were off to a party at Vera's tomorrow night and I shall drown my sorrows in copious amounts of booze, made easier by the fact I only have to walk or crawl two houses up to get home.

Positives: Chris went to Nan's.
Negatives: Tired.

Saturday 31st December 2013

Been shopping, had my nails done and I'm in the mood to *party*!

Sunday 1st January 2014

Happy New Year... Made it back from Vera's alive, kind of. We had a great night with a nice bunch of people. I told everyone we'll throw the next party; Joe had that face, love him. I drank too much, sang too loud and scarily danced like me mum.

Got to bed around four, was back up by five needing tea, was loving the silence of a sleeping house that was soon shattered by the appearance of neighbour Mary. They'd been at the Dog & Duck last night and ever-predictable John had disappeared around eleven. He's told Mary he fancied a drive, turns up at half four this morning with some shit about the car breaking down and that's where he spent the night; my guess is he was tucked up in some tarts bed more like. John the creep, who sometime last year was knocking off some bird, her mother and the aunt. Scumbag. Mary always believes his excuses and so here she was sat on my sofa crying because she feels bad that John saw in the New Year alone in the car in the cold. I like Mary, but she is as thick as shit.

We were supposed to be going round theirs tomorrow night but I've made some old excuse about family popping by. I can't stand that bloke, and with a few bevies under my belt I will tell him so. To look at him gives the rest of us hope: he's 5ft 2, skinny, greasy and has only four teeth. How? What are these women seeing that I don't? He makes my skin crawl. Based on his looks he's got to be either loaded or hung like a mule.

No sooner had Mary left, the brood got up and so the New Year began. Word of advice: *never*- and I mean *never*- forget to lock industrial-strength washing up liquid in a childproof cupboard even if youngest children are in their teens. Tony mistook the bottle for bubble bath (the usual not reading of a label); unbeknown to us he has poured three-quarters of the bottle into the bath. Joe thought it would be hilarious to whip into the bathroom and *steal* the freshly run bath. Entering the bathroom at great speed he has skidded on the copious amounts of foam filling the room, slid and toe-punted the toilet with such force he's cracked the pan. So I then spend the next thirty minutes trying to contain the escaping foam monster, that by now is making its way downstairs, lift an 18 stone man with badly stubbed toes whilst trying to stay upright on a slippery floor, cross-legged through fear of wetting myself laughing, made all the worse by Joe flailing and shouting 'What the fuck's so funny?'

I am now knackered; my back is killing me. On the bright side the hallway and the stair carpet are freshly shampooed. Downside, Joe's laying on the settee with a fish finger between each toe (didn't have any bags of frozen peas) whining like a little girl and giving me evils. I have called a plumber but unless I pay triple cost for a call-out on New Year's day I'll have to wait till Thursday.

So there we have it: day one of 365… *shite!*

Day 3 not looking any better. I'm booked in for a smear test at ten on Monday and the kids like myself have vowed never to eat fish fingers again. Joe, not seeing the funny side of anything, has hobbled off to the study to sulk.

Chloe rang around five this evening, shit the life out of me as she screeched 'Hock I den nooooo!' down the phone. Apparently they had a blinding night. They went to the local village hall gathering; they hummed and arred as to whether or not they should go as they weren't sure they'd be welcome, being the new faces in town, apparently they were. Chloe reckons the Scots do know how to throw a party; or was it Hogmanay? And the next time the village find an excuse to throw another shindig (which can be any excuse from the birth of a new pig to the removal of a plaster), we all have to go. Chloe said it took her back to our days at the Avenue, only without the fit guys. She then apologised for whinging about leaving London fearing that she'd hate it in Scotland and is now convinced she's living in *Brigadoon* and the only thing missing is Gene Kelly dancing on her driveway.

Only a couple of downsides. One: she's nursing the hangover from hell, hasn't got a clue what she was drinking as it seems the spirit bottles don't have labels, feels so rough she's not sure when she'll be able to eat solids again. Yet unbelievably Paul was still up at four to tend to the sheep; unbelievably as he had drank more than Chloe did. Two: although she now believes the change of life was the right move, she's not so sure she finds Paul as attractive as a shepherd, afraid the burly builder she fell in lust with may be fading. How superficial? *Very* lol. xx.

Eye-opener, I do dance like me mum, evidence on Facebook, 'When middle-aged mums go wild'. Thanx Tony. Thanx Chloe for liking and sharing. xx

Paul is in full sympathy with Joe and his foot, whereas Chloe as expected laughed her arse off. She feels that the creation of the foam monster was innocent on Tony's part: poor sod just takes after his father, and blame should lie with Joe childishly stealing baths, adding that with the klutz's track record I'm lucky to have only lost the loo - referring to the time Joe changed a light bulb and shorted out an entire tower block. As for fish fingers, Chloe will also be ridding them from her freezer. I'm looking forward to seeing their farm, more so I can't wait to see the little man in the village who is third-generation postman, bit of an oddball, got a limp and wears a wig but so anal Chloe can rest assured her post will reach her without fail.

No sooner was I off the phone, Elizabeth called. Having told her of my day she dramatically expressed her distress for neighbour Mary, stating firmly in her headmistress voice, 'John's a horrid little man', then recommended she get a good lawyer, followed by, 'Mary should have left him with that disgusting family of women.' In her opinion there is not enough money in the world to coax normal un deprived women to sleep with a weasel like John. With reference to his genitalia, she's yet to meet a man whose size would distract her from the condition of his teeth, albeit four.

Unlike me and Chloe she was 'terribly upset' to hear about Joe's foot, feels he should sue. More shocking for her was that we actually eat fish fingers; followed by, 'Are you in financial difficulties?' *Snob*. As for the damaged 'lavatory' ,she reckons she'd have died if Arthur had broken theirs, as they had their suite imported from Malaysia: 'It's polished volcanic rock.' Seriously!

Told her about going to Scotland on Chloe's invite for the next barn dance; she responds with, 'Myself and Arthur would be honoured to attend the next village gala', adding that they'd be staying in the town rather than the farmhouse, asking if the hotel was five stars. Was about to laugh then she said, 'Not to worry we've stayed in four star before.' I won't lie, I was a bit stunned. Then she says, 'I know Chloe's superficial' -Ooh, lol! Pot, kettle, black - 'but I can't believe that Chloe married Paul for his looks alone.' Proceeded to then lecture me on the advantages of going private for a smear test, putting me right off the cream donut I was munching through.

Having grown bored with slating us she then relayed that New Year for them had been in the company, as expected, of the other directors and their partners, black tie and orchestra as usual. Head honcho Mr Bateman's new wife Tina - or as she's now known, 'the Embryo' on account of her being only a third of his age - made a complete spectacle of herself -'Obviously a girl of her upbringing is not accustomed to drinking champagne. 'She embarrassingly staggered about, flirting the entire evening, until eventually Arthur took it upon himself to escort her to the penthouse, relieving poor Mr Bateman from anymore misery. While she was waiting for Arthur to return the 'wives' explained that they take Pilates lessons to fill the time, as their husbands are always working. They've recommended a chap named Rico who tutors at home. Tells me she was a bit worried as to the looks the ladies exchanged amongst themselves at the mention of his name, so Liz is thinking he may be a 'homosexual'. Arthur has been called away to yet another unexpected meeting, which happens a lot recently, so she has arranged for Rico to come tonight for a consult. Mmm.

Julie arrived here around seven. I filled her in on the girls' conversations, sending her off on one that 'Some things never change!', referring to Elizabeth's snotty attitude about the smear, and that the only difference having it done at a private clinic is the chintzy bleeding curtains and a pot plant: they're still gonna shove the double-headed shoe horn up your crotch, scrape about and leave you feeling like shit. She said that next time she speaks to Liz she's gonna tell her to do us all a favour and ask her private physician to remove the really large plum from her gob and remember she was born and bred in Hackney, for fuck's sake.

We both agreed that Chloe did marry Paul for his looks, or more precisely his forearms. Julie admitted she even found that weird, then said, 'No offence but Joe has the best arse ever', and admitted yes she would go there, if not for the chink in her plan: Joe's not interested. Cheers, mate. Suspicious as ever, Julie asked if Elizabeth had actually looked in Arthur's 'schedule', and why did no one else offer to take the Embryo home? She can't believe that John has the audacity to cheat on neighbour Mary, as God only knows how, as he is repulsive. Don't know what about that statement shocked me more: her dismay at cheating or the fact there is a man she wouldn't sleep with. Julie, like me, loves the sound of Chloe's postman and is betting money that he's got his mother walled up in the basement. As for the next tartan shindig, she'll be there, as it's about time someone puts to rest what a Scotsman wears under his kilt. But unlike 'Eliza Doolittle' she'll be happy to stay on the farm. It's not that she has lower standards than Elizabeth, it's that she's done the maths and has worked out: Hot days + Hard work = Paul and Joe stripped to the waist glistening with sweat. Oh yes, Julie will be there.

Was shocked when she said her New Year plan was to have a quiet dinner with Matt, but being a surgeon he got called away so she picked up a pizza and joined him at the hospital. I was feeling a bit guilty for presuming the worst when she said, 'See, I can do romantic', then drops the 'and by midnight we were shagging in an empty theatre'. There you go, Julie's night did go with a bang. Tonight ended with Julie texting Liz: 'Good luck with Rico, don't think the exchange of looks from the "women that do" were because he's gay. Pilates is that what they call it nowadays, lol'. Then asked me would Joe like her to kiss his toes better? Freak. xx

Positives: Declined the offer to go to the Sunday market with Chris.
Negatives: So gonna miss fish fingers.

Monday 2nd January 2014

Today *has not* gone well… Don't have sex at least 48 hours before a smear test. Nurse shone her light up the never never and with a concerned look asked if I used condoms. Having been sterilized for the past four years I laughed out loud and said, 'Why? Have you found one?' As the words left my lips I'd realised what she'd seen. Shame on me! As I laid there holding the awkward balloon she pulled the smoking card and said, 'It's not good for the cervix to smoke.' I responded, 'It's alright, it aint had a fag in years. 'Why do I say these things? Some sort of nervous disorder I think? Now begins the six-week wait, worrying myself sick for the results. Julie was disappointed when I texted her, she thought I was gonna say they'd found Shergar. Still feel proper shamed, lol.

Only the afternoon and I'm tired. Then again, I was up at five, then the smear. Dunno… just don't feel myself today; actually I've felt a lot like that lately. It's like everything is aggravating me: I have the tolerance of a bear with toothache. I'm not due on, no more stressed than usual and yet grumpy as hell, and I'm tearful.

I rang Chloe, then wished I hadn't: she reckons I'm having a mid-life crisis. I immediately jumped on the defence that MLC was something only little men in big suits have. We ended the call with her snickering her arse off down the receiver. So *if-* and it's only a small '*if* - there's a chance she's right, what's the cure? I went round Julie's for a coffee. She was no better, except she added I was a control freak. She agreed with Chloe then informed me this is why she's never settled down, 'Same shit, different day' and that marriage is like groundhog day, which is why I'm either having a MLC or a breakdown due to boredom of habit. But then she added I could just be mental, as my husband has the best arse ever - even good enough to coax her into nuptials - so says I need to man up. And then asked, 'Can I have him?'She is so not joking. I love Julie dearly but unlike her sister Penny, Julie really is a slut.

In desperation I have emailed Elizabeth, assured that she'll be more diplomatic.

Positives: Kids back at school and Chris opted to have lunch with Abigail rather than bugging me.
Negatives: *Friends.*

Tuesday 3rd January 2014

Connor's 5th birthday.

Presuming there was any foundation to what the others are calling this, this morning I took it upon myself to seek advice on the - let's say - 'minor crisis'. I frantically explained to the librarian the book wasn't for me, before heading home and proving to all that I am *not* having a mid-life crisis.

Note to self: Stop reading books, woman.

All faith has gone. Elizabeth sought advice on my behalf and emailed me a checklist, full of optimism that I could not answer 'Yes 'to any of the questions. I was shot down in seconds.

However it did contain the secret to a full recovery: (1)Have loads of spare cash. (2)Have no dependents. (3)Have no financial responsibilities. (4)Have a very patient and understanding spouse who will let you do whatever you like with whoever you like until this funny phase ends. (1): Nope. (2): Rules me out. (3): In way over my head. (4): Yeah, right. That's me *fucked* then!

Didn't help when Penny arrived late this morning having returned from sunny Malta looking great with the tan, unlike me who's more the tone of an insipid potato. Gutted. Then I get another email from Elizabeth who, if I'm honest, has proper killed me off. Apparently a good description of the MLC is that when you look at your daughter you see the girl you used to be, but when you look in the mirror you see your mother's face staring back. Maybe now's the time to consider getting new friends.

What didn't help was not seeing my grandson today: Andy and Jess decided not to come back from her mum's in Devon until tomorrow. Oh well, that makes a hat trick of two shit sons and their sister. So me and Joe will have to pop round and give Connor his presents then. xx

At least Connor's other Nan gets to see him on his birthday. Hmm, is that bitchy? Give a shit!

Has the world gone mad? The kids have always liked the fact they have quite trendy parents, they have always said how their mates think were cool (all kids think other people's mums and dads are cooler than their own); still, this explains why our house is always full of 17-20-year-olds poncing dinner. Then tonight all hell broke loose as one of Tony's friends dropped a clanger by remarking that I was a MILF? I didn't have a clue what one of them was.

Tony flipped and told him to get out and that he was now barred from the house, whilst relaying that the guy is to never speak to me again. Then Tony turns on me saying, 'Maybe, Mum, you should tone things down a bit and do not speak to any of my mates again.' I haven't got a clue what's happened. What I did know was he's a funny guy. (1)Whose name is on the mortgage deeds? Oh yeah, that'll be me, so sod off round their houses. And (2)don't ever call us parents paranoid and controlling again.

Guessing it had to be some sort of a derogatory remark I texted Julie, the font of all filth, for an explanation. I was quite flattered when she told me what it stood for; don't know if that's a good or bad thing. Julie then asked me for the guy's number as, not having kids herself, she don't see a nineteen-year-old and think 'Oh, I'm old enough to be his mother'; rather, she sees him as fresh meat. Mate, she has no scruples.

After ten minutes of Tony and his mates going on about friendship, loyalty and respect I got in the car to go get some fags when I noticed the note under my windscreen wiper with a number and 'Call me', lol. Whole episode made my day if I'm honest. So what, the comment was vulgar; it was definitely a compliment and most of us haven't heard bullshit like that since we were teenagers. Well, with the exception of Julie that is.

Definitely had too much to drink, yet again. Dunno about mid-life crisis but I'm beginning to think I have a drink problem.

Positives: Alcohol.
Negatives: Alcohol.

Wednesday 4th January 2014

Hairdresser coming at five.

Marie got the pleasure of dropping off her younger sisters at the airport at seven this morning as Molly and Baby head off to stay with their dad in sunny California. Now ensues Chris loitering with too much time on her hands. Oh joy!

Somebody hates me!

New forerunner for depression, MLC has flagged in the shadow of a sinister cloud: I have been diagnosed with alopecia. WTF! Even writing the word makes me want cry, not that I've stopped crying yet. Am I being punished for laughing at men in wigs, or gloating about being a MILF? Baldy Day or B-Day as it will forever be known, as the day that froze my soul.

Having not been badgered by Chris I thought I'd do my hair, so at eleven this morning I'm sat in front of the mirror. I had just finished straightening it when I ran my fingers through and lifted it away from my eyes, and there it was. My heart stopped: it looked like someone had shaved a chunk clean off. After the sick feeling passed which felt like an eternity I searched my pillow, hoping to find evidence of foul play. I didn't. I then sat in silence for fifteen minutes trying to convince myself I'd burnt it off with the straighteners. That wasn't working so I texted Joe and the kids and begged them to confess one of them had done it for a dare while I slept, anything. But no.

I rang the doctors and by the time I was due to be there I'd convinced myself I'd over-dyed it and the prolonged use of straighteners had caused brittle hair that had simply broken off. The doctor calmly took one look at my head and uttered the immortal words 'alopecia Areata', followed by, 'You want to hope it's not the other one. If it is, all your hair will be gone within six weeks.' I thanked him for his kind words, got five steps out the surgery and broke down. I know in my heart I should be grateful it wasn't something more sinister, and that vanity is a sin, but for fuck's sake. Yeah, I said it. Forget about me, but what about my family? How embarrassing for them. I texted them and got varied responses. All included 'we still love you'. Bloody hell, people, I'm going bald, not mutating. Then there was some flannel about 'We'll shave ours off for ya' .Yeah, great, we'll all look like dicks, shall we? (Incidentally that offer was withdrawn twenty minutes later.)

Had to ring the hairdresser and cancel tonight's appointment.

Andy and Jessica did a diversion on the way back from Devon and took the kids to the zoo, so by the time we saw them tonight Connor could barely find the energy to open his presents. But Connor in true form mustered what reserves he had to enquire, 'What's a spam head?'

Note to self: Slap Tony in the mouth.

I'm now going to bed, hoping tomorrow when I awake I'll find this was all a bad dream, or at least wake up and *not* find more hair gone.

Positives: Saved money on haircut.
Negatives: Seriously!

Thursday 5th January 2014

Julie dinner 6pm.

Plumber 11am-5pm.

Aftershock of B-Day, thank God the patch is no bigger. Chris popped in for a coffee and upon hearing the news about my hair sat no nearer to me than 4foot at any given moment. I got a number for a Harley Street hair clinic and spoke to a very nice man who reassured me that my hair will grow back and I probably won't get any more patches, so feeling a tad calmer I searched the net for more information and sadly discovered the reality of this condition is unknown: what will happen how or when. Coupled with pictures I soon realised how lucky I am to have only a small patch. Very humbling.

Also, as stress is believed to be a contributing factor, I've made

17

the decision to accept this condition and keep calm. Great start when Joe said if the patch doesn't re-grow I should have little rabbits tattooed on it... cos from a distance they'll look like hares. Bastard!

Jessica popped by this afternoon after picking Daisy up from nursery. Daisy kept fidgeting and scratching her crotch, Chris left in a panic convinced that Daisy has lice (she was already shaken that alopecia might be hereditary).On further investigation into daisy's drawers I found and removed a chunk of blue tinsel to which Daisy squealed, 'It's for you, Nanny, I puts it there cos I got no pockets. 'I relayed this to Julie at dinner and she reckons Daisy has got good clubbing potential as she herself has been known to place her mobile in the very same place when out. Really? Wouldn't have thought the safest place was in her underwear with the amount of comings and goings on in them. Excuse the pun.

Plumber eventually turned up at seven, new toilet fitted and I'm £200 lighter.

Need to wash hair.

Need the courage to wash hair.

Friday 6th January 2014

Hairdresser 5pm.

Girls' night at Chris's.

Day 3 after B-Day. Never been so terrified as I had to wash my hair this morning. The best solution I felt was to keep both eyes firmly shut -I had no need to see what falls into the bath, thanks- and tried not to shake in my boots when I cleaned out the hairbrush. Think it went well. Then Joe got up after I'd finished, went to clean his teeth, he didn't see the cat asleep under the sink, trod on her tail, she screeched, he screamed (said he didn't),lifted his leg so quickly when he jumped he has dislodged the sink from the wall. Plumber coming back Tuesday. My husband should come with a warning.

On top of that Chris dragged me round B&Q for two hours as she wants to decorate the girls' room while they're away. Well, that was her excuse. I think she wanted to tell me that Penny had been for a pregnancy test this morning, and although the results were negative Chris still enjoyed the gossip. Sad really.

Braved keeping my hair appointment tonight. We talked about anything and everything except baldness, which somehow led me to ask at what age do we women get a blue rinse. Speaking from her experience Carol reckons it's around the seventy-two mark. Shampoo and set starts around seventy, then they get lairy and go for colour. She can't confirm when the wearing of polyester trousers begins, to be worn with the waistband under the armpits. Rain Mac in pink or blue? That probably depends on the colour chosen for the hair, lol.

Much-needed night out and alcohol round Chris's. Everyone was on strict orders beforehand not to mention 'the hair'; it was a good hour I had to endure them staring at my head. We ended up talking about old people and their hair again. Weebles are not my favourite subject. Missed Julie being there as she had flown out to Paris with Charles.

Positives: Eyelids.
Negatives: Joe and plumbing.

Saturday 7th January 2014

Poker night.
Having relayed the conversation about old people's hair last

19

night we'd moved on to what they wear, so this morning several of us went scouring the shops to root out granny clobber. We all see what they wear but never see these articles for sale in shops. The wasted search has led us to unanimously agree that as we found nothing, there must be a little shop in the back of beyond who has the birth records of the British Empire and when someone nears the secret age they receive a 'self-destructing' letter directing them to granny clothing. Further discussion has also brought on the opinion that a similar shop must exist for gay men to purchase them really thick bushy moustaches as they can't be real. Gotta be 'stick on': if they were real, how come straight guys can't seem to grow one, eh? Penny joked that if at forty-odd comes the MLC, at what age should we expect to start smelling of cabbage?

Note to self: Monday go to solicitors and state in will: at first whiff of rotting vegetables mine are to bop me off. Pissy knickers totally acceptable. Er, I wonder if this is why there have been many cases of self-combustion amongst old peeps? Overload of methane, lol. No, not lol. Whole idea of combusting scares me.

Not sure if it's desperation or blind panic: as I have the house to myself tonight I've been surfing the internet for more information on mid-life crisis (better that than alopecia) and what I have discovered is there appears to be a different set of rules for the sexes in a MLC. It's not good for the gander, but very good for the goose. Man has a crisis: he buys a flashy new car, starts dressing like a twenty-something and hooks up with some floozy half his age, egged on and admired by other men. Women: with exception of a few, are in turmoil, riddled with guilt, stuck in the throes of misery, seemingly more concerned they may inflict shame and embarrassment on those closest to them by parading around like a teenager. This, however, may explain those boots I bought last week: black, slinky, high-heeled, knee-length. God, this also explains why the shop assistant gave me that face. The face that said 'Mutton'. Shame on me, lol. Worse still was when the kids saw them and amongst their laughter demanded to know 'Whose are the stripper boots?' Riddled with shame I replied, 'Julie's'. Lucky for me she's still in Paris with Charles, or she'd have defiantly grassed me up. Small mercy on both our parts that I didn't give into the craving to buy that red skimpy dress in Morton's.

Sunday 8th January 2014

Sunday market.

Very strange! I cooked a perfect roast today, or so I thought. Everything looked perfect until I bit into a roast potato. I can't describe what it tasted like; Joe agreed it was more of a physical response than a flavour, declaring it made his mouth screw up like an arsehole. Still, he ate them though. But given my run of luck at the moment I did *not*. Weird?

This evening I've found myself feeling quite weepy again and wishing Granddad was still here; he'd make me feel better. I owe almost everything to the advice and wisdom passed onto me from my grandparents. I remember the look on Granddad's face when I asked him if he was gonna get himself one of them golf cart things: 'They're for lazy bastards and old people' was the response. Element of truth in that, I believe. Retirement didn't stop him from getting up early, walk to the shop to get his newspapers, do a bit of gardening and outdoor work for a local factory; that's what he meant by lazy, get idle and waste away. Same applies to Nan: she's never stopped. Before Granddad died she was always visiting people in hospital. What shocked me was she didn't know half of them, but as they had no family of their own she would visit them, buy them magazines and chat. Thus came my phobia of Ribena, as I was taken on so many of these

Samaritan visits and was forced to drink it as every patient had a bottle of the bleeding stuff. Gross. Once they were discharged, Nan would visit them at home too, helping out with housework or ironing. She told me it was because' They're old': I found out she was actually ten years older than most of them.

So, old peeps' buggies? To be fair they are a brilliant invention, giving freedom and independence to people who generally need help getting about. These ones we recognise because they drive with consideration and care, not the ones who will mow down anyone from a embryo upwards on public paths; bet these are the same miserable arseholes who forced the law for cyclists to ride on roads. Ironically, 99% of cyclists of all ages I've encountered on a path have slowed down or stop to let you pass; I've never had one honk like a maniac, speed up or verbally attack me. Clue's in the title, people: *foot*path. In my day of pram pushing I never expected anyone to hold open doors for me, was always grateful when someone did offer; wielding a pram never gave me the right to jump queues, cross roads without looking, and I certainly never bombed down supermarket aisles knocking over displays and small children.

With the exception of a few, like my grandparents, 'old people': nope, don't like them. And when all the good ones have passed away, with them will go the contents of the 'survival kit' handbag. Nan's bag contains everything you'd need in an emergency: knicker elastic with threader (stirring sticks pilfered from cafes), bar of soap (pinched from hotel in Benidorm), never-ending tissues, pens, shoelace, mini sewing kit, screwdriver, tweezers, safety pins, teaspoon, headscarf that always smells like face powder, crepe bandage, plasters, painkillers, coupons carefully cut from magazines they always forgot to trade in. Newspaper clippings from 1952. Packet of seeds. Endless.

My personal favourite are the boiled sweets that lurk in the abyss for centuries and when you try and unwrap them you can't tell which is cellophane or sweet as they've merged over time as one, so then you have to suck it, picking plastic off your tongue as you go along. There was, however, one item in the handbag that would send a ripple of dread through every child: the rolled-up plastic see-through bonnet. I used to start crying as the first raindrop fell. For me there was the added bonus that if there was more than a drizzle, my Nan has a rolled up matching Mac. I've never seen Nan with a cook book; nah, it's all from memory – and given some of the weird concoctions she's fed us it's probably better that we didn't know the ingredients. They tasted nice, and ignorance is bliss so they say. I was always impressed with her winter soup: eat canned crap and half an hour later your stomach thinks your throat's been cut; Nan's would fill you up even without bread and was available anytime, night or day. What I didn't know back then was it is a soup that gets topped up over a couple of months, use-by dates not applicable then.

We would get told off for climbing trees or scrumping, until it was jamming season: then we got sent up cherry trees and told to raid the orchards. Being scared of the dark was unacceptable in any grandparents' eyes; truth behind that was, good or bad, all old people are to bloody tight to leave a light on all night. Pointless to complain if it was cold in their house: hell would freeze over before they'd put the fire on; the best we got was for them to put on the illusionary flame effect to which they would say 'That's better'. Mind you, they also said don't paint a room blue as it makes it colder, and I've found that to be true. Old people confused the shit out of us little kids: 'Take your coat off, you won't feel the benefit. 'Do you need the toilet? No? Well, go anyway.'

If someone asked Nan what time the bus came at the top of our street, she could recite the entire schedule off by heart. Why, then, was she always running for the bus, dragging me so fast my feet dangled behind, thus causing my little legs to be tired, and then once on the bus why, if it was crowded, did she make me stand up so someone else could sit down? Then on arrival at the destination would whip out an old hanky, give it a lick, then wipe your face then force you to blow your nose then check each nostril to be sure you had no bats in the cave.

You were a big girl's blouse if you cried: told us our cut knees didn't hurt when they clearly did. Back-chatting was a criminal offence, yet in the next breath told us to stand up for ourselves. I've pulled many a face into the changing wind and it never stayed that way. Where's all the wool they accused me of pulling over their eyes?

Lol, good memories. Feel much better. Looking forward to bed.

Confession: Did buy that red skimpy dress in Morton's. xx

Monday 9th January 2014

Joe football.

Shopping.

Got up this morning feeling quite perky and with the kids at their dad's Chris is starting the decorating in their bedroom today, thus leaving me in peace for a while. Bonus xx

Called Elizabeth: she's been to some LIFE seminar, paid real money for some ponce to make her feel like she was inadequate and weak. As one of her closest friends I assured her we can do that for her and it wouldn't cost her a penny.

Tony and his mates have gone for a takeaway tonight; Leigh's gone to a club and Joe's at football, so I have total peace and quiet for at least ten minutes this evening. Lovely. xx

Bored, bored, having paced the house looking for something to do I opted for raiding the fridge and have just consumed one and a half boxes of chocolate fingers. Feeling rather green around the gills. xx

Speaking of fingers, people claim to see many things in vomit that they don't remember eating but nobody notices the finger that lurks in the cold sick that as soon as you go to clean it up the skin that's formed on top breaks, releasing the digit which shoots straight down your throat, making you gag.

Having now eaten everything that weren't nailed down, boredom soon got the better of me again, so I thought I'd brave the situation and have a good look at the 'bald patch'.

Note to self: Don't do it again, luv!

Tuesday 10th January 2014

Plumber 6pm.

Not sure what takeaway Tony went to last night but I will *not* be eating from there, he has the worse gas ever. The plumber returned and has reaffixed the sink to the wall. What he charges, he should change his name to Dick Turpin.

Slung stripper boots in wardrobe, momentarily paused to conclude that I can't win: if I start dressing like a stereotypical middle-aged mum the kids are gonna say I'm an embarrassment, yet if I commit to urges and dress trendy and young (and it's a serious urge) they're gonna say I'm an embarrassment. Yeah, well. It's a two-way street sometimes: the way they dress is embarrassing, fashionable or not, and why do daughters sneer at the clothing we buy for ourselves with the 'Alright for someone your age, I wouldn't be seen dead in it!'. Why, then, does same said article find its way into her wardrobe? No point retrieving the item now as you can't wear it through fear of being accused of wearing your daughter's clothing, which is rather 'sad'.

Made a constructive decision to be calm: MLC, worrying about smear results, all stress I don't need if I'm going to avoid more balding of the head.

Mum called, Cousin Karen had her smear results through Friday, they came back abnormal. Cheers, Mum. They wanted to see Karen again in three weeks. Fearing the worst, as we all do, she demanded they see her immediately; they informed her there were no sooner appointments so Karen said she'd pay. She was seen that evening by the same doctor who wasn't available without a fee. Not looking good for the doctor. Her Gary gets let out two weeks from now and I've got a funny feeling he's about to break his parole. Thanx again, Mum. xx

Wednesday 11th January 2014

Went to see how Chris was getting on with the decorating. Don't know why I thought she'd be doing it herself: materials and labour all billed to secret daddy, as usual. As a sixteen-year-old groupie she may not have got her man, but she did get five of his eight children: all conceptions match UK tour dates, lol. Still, at least it's always been amicable, his wife and other kids have never had a problem with it, so happy families all round and none of them have ever wanted for anything.

Called Chloe and they're making a start on the restoration of the farmhouse this week. Pauls made friends with their neighbour Derek and will be popping over to his farm, 7 acres away, as Derek is letting him borrow his ram Titan. Apparently he'll hump anything. The ram, not Derek. At least I think that's right. With this offer they could double their stock within a year. Very generous.

Tony's gut rot has progressed to hideous. Wallpaper is starting to peel.

Chloe called this morning, restoration commenced. Paul ripped out all the carpets and to their surprise uncovered the most beautiful wooden floors; she gave them a mop and they've retained all the original lustre. Wooden floors would be great for Chloe to brush up her tap dancing just in case Gene does appear.

We are now referring to Tony's guts as the 'Grim', cos it is. Will not - and I mean will not - ever eat fried chicken from a fast food establishment. If that stench hasn't subsided by tomorrow I'm taking him to hospital. Thank god we don't have a canary.

Not had much sleep as Chris was calling me from the airport this morning: Friday the 13th and Chris's nerves were shot to shit as Molly and Baby were flying home from California. I will never get how she bagged herself a pop star. I managed to doze back off when I was woken by a frantic call from Chloe: she's woken up covered in large red itchy lumps. I wake up every morning with one of them and it snores.

Ooh, mystery of dodgy roast potatoes solved. Joe told me we had no cooking oil left, I told him it was in the usual place, after another look he declared 'Nope, only a bottle of lime cordial.' That explains the flavour and the physical response to the spuds.

Luckily for Tony the 'Grim' seems to have gone; it was so bad I thought we were gonna have to enlist the help of the Vatican as it was nothing short of a demonic possession.

Saturday 14th January 2014

Leg wax 2pm.

As we're babysitting tonight we have Baby and Molly too, so Chris has gone to dinner at Abigail's. Rang Chloe to see how she was and the itching has become unbearable. She's been to the doctor and he suggested it could be bites. Then asked her if their bed was old. Insulted she told him he'd a bloody cheek, as they were all brand new, so now he's ruling out bed bugs. Still, on return to the farm Chloe has immediately hoovered all the mattresses and trailed through a pile of dead skin flakes to put her mind at rest. I thought she took it well, considering we're talking bed bugs. Errgh, dunno about hovering the mattress, I'd have torched the joint.

Note to self: Where it concerns Chris, this conversation did *not* happen.

Sunday 15th January 2014

Chris picked up the girls around ten and headed off to Nan's.

I needed to change a plug so I headed for the one place for such a job: The Crap Drawer! Every home has one, filled to the brim with loose change, old playing cards, odd toy pieces, drawstring from old track pants, and let's not forget the random compasses that prick your finger every time you start rummaging. It's just all crap, you can never find what you thought was in there, then you can't shut it. You have to reach in, pushing all the shit to the back, So's you can close the drawer, which never works and the drawer has to be left open by an annoying inch.

Monday 16th January 2014

Joe football.

Shopping.

Another frantic call from Chloe this morning: her lumps are multiplying in amount and size, she says she can feel things crawling on her skin but she can't see anything. Paul thinks she's losing the plot and is at present waiting for a reply from the soap powder company, having contacted them in the hope they've changed the ingredients. Logic tells me they haven't, but I'll let Chloe live in hope. Unlike Elizabeth, who emailed Chloe last night with the opinion that the trauma of the move is the cause and suggested Chloe should see a psychiatrist.

Chris appeared after lunch following her usual Monday jaunt to the doctors. Two weeks ago she showed me a lump on her elbow, stating it was a mole that looked funny. On closer inspection I'd told her it looked funny because it was a wart. Not happy with my blasé diagnosis, to the doctor she has gone and here she sat in tears because he'd told her it was 'human papilloma virus'. Took me two minutes on the internet and much patience to prove it's the medical name for a *wart*. In the end I had to call Mum for back-up. She arrived with a sirloin, rubbed it on the *wart*, then buried the meat in the garden. Little does Chris know that twenty minutes after she left mine I saw Mutley run off with the freshly dug-up steak, and I'm in no mood to explain to Chris that it's only a placebo, as I can guarantee she'll think I'm talking about the garden shade and that I've developed a speech impediment, which will bring on a whole new set of panics.

Tuesday 17th January 2014

Car MOT 11am.

Excellent customer service: not only did they return Paul's call but the soap company have asked them to email a photo of the lumps with a full description of symptoms, which they will pass onto their dermatology department. Hmm, either they do have fantastic customer care or they know something we don't.

Sarah's been barred from London transport because of an old biddy: some guy had got up to give her his seat on seeing she was heavily pregnant, and this old woman has shoved past Sarah and parked her arse on the seat. The guy told her she was bang out of order which triggered off a riot of old people tutting and sniping how the younger generations have no manners or respect. Sarah pointed out that if our generation had behaved like them we'd have got a back-hander from our elders. The inspector being as old as the rest of them, banned Sarah. Still that's not as bad as the time Mum saw a pregnant woman faint near the exit doors, the driver stopped, and before he could help the Weebles were tutting and stepping over her to get off the bus, as God forbid they miss their stop.

Old people make me sick.

Connor's class presentation 9am.

Connor has once again become the focus of everyone's attention. At his class Open Day he was chosen to tell the story of Sleeping Beauty, aided in pictorial form by his classmates. Narrating and pointing to posters depicting each passage he reaches the one that has but one thing drawn on it – the size and shape was already raising a few smiles amongst the younger parents when Connor proudly says in the clearest and loudest voice, 'This is the prick and Beauty touched it.' Obviously a poorly drawn needle, funny as hell, which escalated to hilarious as with arms folded across his chest and a pout he shouted, 'Aint funny, it hurt Beauty when it went in!'

Soap people contacted Chloe this afternoon and according to their specialist the lurgy is being caused by too much histamine being released into her system. They have advised she call the Environmental Health and if all else fails they have offered to have her tested at an allergy clinic free of charge.

Mutley vets 9am

Chloe rang the Environmental Health this morning, she explained what's been happening and somewhere amongst the blokes' laughter they came round to the farm. Unofficial diagnosis: Chloe is mental. Professional opinion was that when Paul ripped out the carpets something got released in the dust that didn't like her, hence the allergic reaction. House has now been sprayed. Still, we had a good laugh remembering when Elizabeth's sister had a rat in her loft: Environmental would have come out for free but she opted to pay £300 because the company she booked assured her they didn't have anything written on their vans, thus hiding from the neighbours what they had come to do. When they pulled up, true to their word there was no logo plastered on the vehicle. Instead there was a 2 foot fibreglass cockroach on its roof.

Friday 20th January 2014

Shopping with Julie 9am

Went shopping with Julie and I saw a really nice dress in the sale: it screamed my name, right up to the moment I tried it on and I looked like crap. Obviously made in mind for a woman with a DDD chest, and considering I have breasts like spaniel's ears I put it back on the rack. Isn't getting stretch marks sacrifice enough for bringing life into this miserable world? Made more miserable by Julie pointing out hers were still as pert as they were twenty years ago. Yeah, well, that's cos she bought them that way.

Phoned Chloe again: the lumps are finally going down. Paul's ripping out the last of the carpets today so Chloe's off out all day through fear of being eaten alive again. God, I hope they make sure all flooring is gone before Chris goes for a visit, Gods in Heaven forbid she actually caught something real.

Saturday 21st January 2014

Girls' night Tina's 7pm.

Spent the evening around Tina's, several of us accompanied

by even more bottles of wine. We were having a great evening until we convinced Tina she would look good in Julie's new 6inch heels, so one minute she was parading up and down the upstairs hallway admiring herself in the mirror, the next instant: gone. *Who* in their right mind has a mirror on the wall at the top of the stairs? She tumbled down the stairs for what seemed a lifetime before laying in a heap at the bottom, with blood coming from a split lip. At the sight of claret, Chris has passed out. Julie had to be restrained as she began shouting, 'Hope you haven't scuffed my heels!' I was as usual to be found on the floor, screaming with laughter. Among the madness we did manage to call Terry, who carted her off to hospital accompanied by Julie. Not sure if she went for Tina's benefit or cos she didn't want to let her new shoes out of her sight. Chris made a full recovery when Penny threw a handful of cold water in her face. Great night. xx

Sunday 22nd January 2014

Was quite happily sleeping off last night's crate of wine when I was woken by a blood-curdling scream this morning. I ran out into the street where neighbours from both sides were standing on Mary's driveway. From within she was screaming 'Please help me!' Joe immediately kicked the door in and I rushed past him, my heart in my throat, and Joe in tow we entered her lounge. She was stood still with all the colour gone from her face, crying. She slowly points to her left leg and whispered between sobs, 'There's a mouse up my trousers.' So kneeling down I carefully slid my hand up her trouser leg and grabbed the warm soft critter. I pulled it out to discover it was actually a rolled-up pair of tights that must have got caught up in her laundry. I turned to show Joe but he was nowhere to be seen – so much for hero. I then spent the next half-hour trying to regain the strength in my legs and stop my hands shaking from the adrenalin rush that always comes after panic has passed.

Monday 23rd January 2014

Joe football.

Shopping with Chris 10am.

Was supposed to be going up town this morning, then Chris cancelled on me. I spoke to mum about half an hour later and she said Chris had phoned, mumbling something about unguis incarnates. Knowing my sister is not bright enough to have learnt to speak fluent Latin, or witchy incarnations... nope, she's been to the doctors again. Oh surprise, surprise: alright, Cilla, lol. It is in fact an ingrown toenail. I'm beginning to think the doc gives her the scary names on purpose for his own amusement, good old boy. Believe me, there is nothing funnier than fear on someone's face and Chris makes it so easy. Bless her.

How can scissors vanish? No matter how many I buy – and that's easily got to be 50 pairs over the years – I can only ever find the one pair that was blunted by the kids. Perhaps they're in the 'safe place'? Where is that, again? We all go there and squirrel away our prized possessions for safe-keeping but somehow its whereabouts always eludes us. As hard as I try I cannot think of anywhere in this bloody house that's big enough to be hoarding all the things I've stowed away that could be invisible to the eye.

Called Elizabeth. Oh, how funny is she? Always complaining

she never has a minute to herself, charity luncheons (offloading guilt for lavish spending), seminars on life coaching (simple: just get a grip, luv), tennis, spa treatments, dance lessons, to name but a few... but cookery classes? What's the point of the live-in chef? She did mention that Arthur's been away all weekend on business, so maybe I'm being a bit harsh and these things she does keeps the loneliness at bay.

Tuesday 24th January 2014

Paul has bought a turkey chick to be fattened and consumed Christmas, aww.

Penny popped in lunch time; apparently Chris had a meeting with Baby's teacher this morning. It seems Baby has been enlightening everyone in her class how she met Bon Jovi when he came for a visit at her Dad's house. The school don't allow the telling of tales, Chris has had to agree to speak to Baby about her active imagination. Déjà vu: when Marie was little she told her classmates she'd spent the weekend on Elton John's yacht. If only they knew.

Leigh got back from shopping earlier, armed with several bags full of new outfits. I eagerly awaited the unveiling (a little too eager, I think) of the latest trend. Knowing I would probably wish I was twenty years younger, the reality was worse than anticipated as I saw clearly the same fashion had come round again, and for me it was the third time I'd seen it: not only as a teen, but still hanging in my wardrobe, thus highlighting that my clothes were as old as my kids.

Christine's 43rd birthday.

Accompanied by Julie and Tina we took Chris shopping, then for a manicure and facial. We had lunch, got back about four, and by eight o'clock we were at the Dog & Duck where Chris preceded to cover every gay anthem on the karaoke list. Chris had a good birthday overall and we got through the day without hiccups, and where that concerns Chris it is a very large bonus. Julie pulled some whelp; damn, she's impressive to watch, as she actually does nothing and men gravitate toward her.

The weather's been horrendous all day. Andy called about four to say they've decided to stay over another day in Yarmouth as the roads are not safe to drive on. Not sure what possessed them to take the take the kids to a water park in January. Gets it off his father.

Chris asked me to pick the girls up from school as she's feeling under the weather; not bloody surprised after last night's obliteration of the Dog & Duck's bar stock.

Jeni and Jaki have arrived safely at the farm this morning. It will be nice for Chloe as the girls live in America, which means her and Paul don't see them as much as they'd like.

Julie came round to relay the grubby details of the whelp. Can't help but admit the idea of an affair sounds exciting, but in all honesty - let's forget for a moment that I love Joe and wouldn't want to hurt him - I couldn't be asked, I have neither the time nor the energy, the MLC is just a very awkward time between life and death. Not that I'm having one.

Hairdresser 5pm.

Andy and Jess arrived home from Yarmouth around three, safe and sound.

I had to force Joe to have his hair cut today. What is it with men? They're either over-immaculate or damn right scruffy. Apparently he doesn't like the way the hairdresser pulls he's head around. WTF, man up, mate!

Why did I have to force him? Surely he's supposed to make an effort to appear attractive to me?

Joe, still miffed for having to go to the barbers, has taken great pleasure in reminding me that my roots need doing as all my grey is showing. Childish. I used to complain about going grey young but a dose of alopecia teaches you to love whatever hair you have. It's Mum's family that passes the premature hair colour; to think I used to joke that it could have been worse and I'd taken after Dad and gone bald. Not funny now.

Is it me, or does everyone else seem so much younger than me?

No Julie about this weekend: she's gone away with Danny, he being the boss of the rival law firm. He's so arrogant he actually thinks she knocks about with him for his looks; it's not a coincidence then that 2% of his clients have been scouted to her firm since she's been seeing him.

Sunday market.

I have come to the conclusion that there is no sexier smell than that of fresh washing. After all these years, Joe still thinks it's a little weird that I sniff the laundry as I empty it from the machine, when I hang it on the line, and after I iron it. Hmm, maybe I am a little weird.

Chris has gone to the Sunday market. I await her return with my nice greasy pineapple fritter.

Joe football.

Shopping.

Christine went to the doctors at the crack of dawn this morning after noticing a dry patch on the back of her hand, being the acute worrier she is and none too bright. When the doctor said she had scabies she flipped and shouted, 'I ain't never been on a boat!' By the time she'd rung me approx. fifteen minutes later after leaving the surgery she had already consumed six oranges. Whilst trying to console her amid my Snickers she then confessed she'd written to an agony aunt enquiring about assisted suicide, no less, lol. How sad when she has us. Wished I hadn't rung Elizabeth, she's now asking if mental illness runs in my family. She bollocked me for laughing as I should be a little more concerned as to the state of my sister's mind, as this could be a cry for help. Chloe as ever sprang to my defence with the 'state the obvious': Chris is and always will be a neurotic hypochondriac. Only then asked: did my mum have an affair? As the rest of my family are not like that. Then wet herself laughing as the penny dropped concerning the six oranges and the boat: that Chris had thought the doctor meant scurvy. What a div !

Note to self: Must ask Mum if she did have an affair.

Tuesday 31st January 2014

Mum's for lunch 12pm.

Met Mum for lunch. Sadly no affair. Mum also said none of us should worry about Chris needing assistance to end her own life, as she believes Chris will worry herself dead long before needing a one-way ticket to Switzerland.

Mmm pie 'n mash for dinner covered in lovely oozy green liquor. Joe will no doubt stare in disbelief as me and the kids devour our favourite meal; he thinks it's disgusting. You haven't lived, buddy. This is the same man who eats jam and cheese sandwiches, skank.

Wednesday 1st February 2014

Hairdresser 5pm.

Chris has rushed to the doctors again this morning; she'd had the fright of her life when she'd passed blood. Diagnosis: piles, probably brought on by all the fruit she's been eating, lol. The doctor has assured her she wouldn't be needing a transfusion. Chloe nearly died laughing when I called her and Elizabeth on the other hand has informed me that bleeding can be a sign of something very serious and it's by far not a laughing matter. Alright, Gloomy Glad, fuck's sake. Does she ever see the funny side of anything? Apart from hypocondriacitus Chris has got bugger all wrong with her, serious or non-serious.

Leigh had a look at 'the bald patch' with a magnifying glass, sadistic little mare. She insisted she can see tiny black stubbly hairs. Thank the gods; words cannot express how good that was to hear.

Thursday 2nd February 2014

Window cleaner.

Thought Daisy was the cutest thing this afternoon, having raided the fridge of chocolate aided and abetted by Connor she was dancing round the kitchen and in the cutest voice kept saying 'Kit Kat, Kit Kat' and pointing at her cheeky face. Ten minutes later and still mumbling I noticed she was pointing at her nose not her mouth, stunned disbelief followed the discovery of a ball of foil from pilfered confectionary well and truly lodged up her left nostril. I fear Daisy may have inherited Chris's defective gene, having done the same herself when she was six.

We have a mouse somewhere in this house. I have spent the last hour searching the house to no avail. Joe's arguing with me, saying it's the washing machine or the tumble dryer squeaking. Although neither appliance has been on today. He had a nervous look in his eyes, me thinks he may be scared of wee rodents.

40

Dentist 9am.

Girls' night Abigail's.

Popped in Chris's on the way back from the dentist, she was sat on one of the kid's old rubber rings and there was a faint aroma of TCP emanating from her. Only stayed a little while as I began to feel that if I remained it was a matter of time before I would either laugh and take the piss, or punch her in the head for being such an imbecile. She better not bring the 'ring' round Abigail's tonight.

Why don't quilt covers fit? Single, double, king size, don't matter. You always have 6inches of excess material on one side serving no other purpose than to wrap around your feet while you sleep, entrapping your legs, causing you to wake in the night in a blind panic.

No sign of the 'ring' tonight, instead we watched her shuffle about like an eighty-year-old .I don't suffer with this ailment so on reflection maybe I'm being a little harsh. Given that the arse is watertight, to be having something stuck neither in nor out must be agony. The equivalent of putting your wedding ring round your wrist, lol. Got to smart a bit.

Patrick 37th birthday.

It seems I've finally got me head together after all these years and now the body is falling apart. A simple thing like brushing my hair(what's left of it): I couldn't help but notice in the mirror that my arms were wobbling, at which point Tony walked past and said, 'Nice bingos Mum.'

Joe and the others are all at Flannigan's tonight for his brother's birthday.

Sunday market.

Woke up with the right hump this morning. Unlike my sister I'm talking about my mood not an overnight curvature of the spine. I went to bed with a migraine, finally got to sleep around two when I was woken again by Joe crashing about in the fridge on return from Flannigan's with a severe case of the munchies. I haven't got a clue what time I got back to sleep but woke again around six feeling like I couldn't breathe, only to discover Joe's arm slumped across my chest. What's the point of having a bed 6 foot by 5 foot when you're both going to lay on 3 foot of it? I was sick of my own company by seven so I rang Chris and told her I'd meet her at the Sunday market. Surprisingly she hadn't developed any new ailments and the morning was quite pleasant. Chris needed to pop in the supermarket to grab some bits she'd offered to cook for Charlie's birthday party tomorrow.

All was well until we got to the checkout where we were met by the most sour-faced individual, sulkily scanning each item then practically throwing them to the end where Chris was waiting to pack. I politely asked (Chris said I didn't), 'Were you forced to work here?' *'Nah.'* 'Then why the fucking attitude then? If you hate the job so much, if it's too beyond you to be polite and professional, then fucking leave.' Not sure if this is what drew the attention of the store manager, or my heightened outburst at Chris as she cowered and stupidly said, 'Ssshhhh, you're making a scene.' I vaguely remember screaming at Chris to 'Man up!' and it all went a bit screwy from there. All I know is she got her shopping for free.

Monday 6th February 2014

Charlie's 5th birthday party.

Joe football.

Chris has a gammy armpit: lumpy, itchy and sore, pretty grim, known in the trade as an ingrown hair. What's with her at the moment? Everything's growing in. First the toenail, now the hair; too bloody tight to give anything away that girl.

Mate, hope there's no vol-au-vents at the party, lol.

Charlie's party was fun: Penny had hired a magician. Joe watched intensely as trick after trick was performed, wide-eyed and intensely gripped. I remarked on this observation. Looking a bit embarrassed he replied, 'Oh, I wasn't really watching, I was lost in thought.' If that was true then he was in very unfamiliar territory.

Elizabeth has been away on yet another tennis weekend with the Stepford Wives; starting to feel a bit sorry for them all. For all Joe's faults I wouldn't want to be just passing ships.

Tuesday 7th February 2014

Shopping.

Cinema.

Watched *Meet the Spartans* on a rerun at the cinema, under sufferance as I thought it was gonna be an all-out macho film.

I was pleasantly surprised, as it was a spoof. Thought it was the funniest thing I've seen for a long while, until it was topped by Joe mimicking the Spartans skipping all the way home, which took forever as I laughed myself almost to death. Leigh said she heard me from the end of the driveway, then looked a bit dumb when we'd said we'd been to the pictures, followed with, 'Seriously showing your age. No one calls it that no more: it's the cinema, Mum.'

Wednesday 8th February 2014

Road tax due.

Joe dentist 10am.

Interesting conversation with Julie about 'road tax': apparently it was abolished in 1937 and is actually 'car tax'. Me and many others are under the illusion that this money goes to maintaining roads and it's clearly not: so where is it going? And why are some not paying? Its proper name is 'vehicle excise duty', still referred to as 'road tax' as it's apparently easier to say. Hmm, road tax contains seven letters, car tax only six, so I'm not believing that excuse. So where is this money going? It does, however, explain these residential parking tickets: Joe protests every year at the fact he pays 'road tax' but still has to pay on top to park the car out the front of the house. Clearly it's got nothing to do with the road, it's worse than that: we're paying 'car tax' for owning a vehicle, then having to pay again to park it. Thieving, lying, bastards.

Oh mate, I need a life. xx

Car insurance due.

Still pissed off about the 'car tax', now gotta part with more money for insurance, no doubt that's gone up again cos of all the ones who are driving without any, and having accidents.

Was thinking earlier how attractive my husband is, Mmm.

Chloe arriving today.

Chris rang me from the hospital this morning: she had fainted on the Tube this morning and at least someone had the decency to call an ambulance (that's cos old people only use buses).On assessment at the emergency department the doctor noticed her notes had shown her many recent visits to her GP so they thought it best to run some blood tests; the results have shown that she'd overdosed on vitamins! Having cut down on the fruit intake (didn't want piles back) she'd compensated, or so she thought, by taking treble doses of vitamins. Seriously, if she had brains she'd be dangerous.

We're off to Chloe's grandparents' 50th anniversary party at Lloyds Lodge tomorrow. Fifty years looking at the same face every day, hands up to Betty and Alfred: but how? There is already the question as to will I be doing my party trick of choking on a mouthful of trifle, causing a grape to wedge up behind the nasal cavity, thus causing severe pressure from coughing to force grape to come out of my nostril whole, regardless of immense pain. The saga has become somewhat a legend, so that so-called family and friends live in hope of a repeat performance.

Chloe should be here by four and we're going round Julie's for dinner tonight. Shame Elizabeth couldn't come, we were blown out for the Batemans' weekend garden gala. Know where I'd rather be.

Sunday 12th February 2014

Sunday market.

On entering the Lodge last night I thought I'd walked into my worst nightmare as the room was filled with silver hair. Reassured slightly as no whiff of wet cabbage in the air, only the aroma of lavender water and carbolic, yet still a combined age of 2,000, dare I say. The truth is we had a blinding night, lol. The old birds danced more than us, very amusing the unanimous two steppers, the repeated lifting of the skirt to flash the knickers, not sure knickers is the right word though, in the 80s we called them 'clam diggers' and they were worn over the knickers.

Betty's younger sister at eighty-four wouldn't leave Joe alone all night; he says he was humouring her – clearly not, pal, she was more his pace I think. Aww, poor old git.

Chloe left for Scotland at seven this morning, heading home to the prairie. It's done me the world of good seeing her this weekend.

Monday 13th February 2014

Joe football.

Elizabeth called me late last night. Her and Arthur had

spent the weekend at Mr Bateman's estate which ended terribly. Mr Bateman's late wife has a Persian Blue cat named Humphrey, a very spoilt creature. The Embryo after much begging and pouting convinced Mr Bateman To buy her a Chihuahua. Apparently since the arrival of Bridget, Humphrey has been sulking, refusing to eat and hiding out in the kitchen, not amused that Bridget has taken his place on the master bed and he's been shut out because Embryo thinks he'll attack the dog, who is three times smaller than the cat. Riddled with guilt of his late wife's memory, Mr Bateman felt the animals have had long enough to get used to each other and left the bedroom door open Saturday night. Sunday morning, Embryo awoke to find a medium blood stain, one little paw and a few splinters of bone. As much as I dislike gold diggers I couldn't help but feel for the girl. Thankfully Arthur was on hand as he seemed to be the only person who could console her. Hmm?

Picked up Charlie, Rhianne, Baby and Molly from school. Penny, Chris and Abigail went swimming. On dropping off Charlie and Rhianne I stayed for a coffee and Mark came home with flowers. Penny was overjoyed; didn't impress me much, they were clearly from a garage, and the only reason men buy them from there is forgotten birthdays, anniversaries or a guilty conscience for something they've done.

Valentine's tomorrow

Wednesday 15th February 2014

Rico arrived at Elizabeth's for her first Pilates consultation last night; first impressions were very good, as was his English. Lizzie is guessing he must be top of his field as his diary was booked full, so thinks him squeezing her in must be that he has seen potential in her. Such an attentive young man, very focused, she believes that whatever he went after he would get.

She aint getting it, is she? Lol.

Joe bought me a massive bunch of flowers and we went to dinner for Valentine's.

My brain is screaming 'Yes!' but my body can't be asked. What's going on with my sex drive?

Thursday 16th February 2014

Why is it that I pay to have the house phone ex-directory? Oh, that's right, so I don't get unwanted calls from random's. Then pray do tell why I get repeated calls from salesmen? *No*, I do not want double glazing or solar panels, I don't use credit cards, clearly haven't won a prize for a competition I didn't enter. Mate!

Feeling a bit bad right now! Chris has caught the arse end of the mood the telesales men had put me in. She called this afternoon in a panic to tell me she was eating cherries and had accidently swallowed the stone, looking for some small measure of reassurance that she'd be OK. To which I replied, 'You will be only if it doesn't take root in your gut.' Mum called me three hours later and had a right go at me, as no sooner had Chris hung up than she'd had her fingers down her throat repeatedly until she'd thrown it up.

Roll on Friday: Joe and the boys are all going Flannigan's for Mark's 33rd birthday and we're all at Penny's.

Dad's birthday.

Girls' night was fun last night. About an hour into the conversation Penny tells us Rhianne and Charlie have gone down with chicken pox. Shockingly Chris didn't bat an eyelid, declaring that our lot have all had it and you can only get it once. Mean as it was, the look on her face when Tina said 'You could get shingles though'. Julie followed up with, 'And if the spots meet in the middle it means death.' I'm laughing now, but any money says Chris *will* get shingles, they *will* meet in the middle, and I *will* have Mum on my case again. I'm cooking dinner for Dad's 63rd birthday tonight. I guess time will tell.

Dinner was going really well until for dessert I produced the Black Forest gateau and Chris went off on one, accusing me of taking the piss with the cherries. Lucky for her I'd had too much wine or maybe I wouldn't have seen the funny side and laughed. It all escalated when Dad chuckled along with me, and Mum exploded at him with some shit about Chris being a vulnerable girl. Hmm, why the sympathy suddenly for her hypochondria? Maybe there was an affair after all, lol. xx

Stab in the dark here, but I'm guessing Chris is still angry with me. I was up at six this morning waiting for her to pick me up to go Sunday market; I was still waiting at seven. Shame on me, lol.

Note to self: From now on, no more laughing at Chris.

I saw on the news a women escaped jail for shoplifting because the lawyer claims she's a kleptomaniac. I'm guessing the difference between being one of these or just a thief is that they're not doing it on purpose for gain. Who am I to argue? But it seems very strange that kleptomaniacs are always middle or upper class; never heard of a poor person being one.

Monday 20th February 2014

Chris has surfaced, all sweetness and light, as I knew she would, lol. It's Monday and she's been to the doctors. She goes on to say she won't be drinking again as the doctor has said she has psoriasis. The last thing I heard was the front door slam accompanied with 'Heartless bitch' as I felt the tears roll down my cheeks, pml.

Joe came home with a smile, presented me flowers. Not sure why. And as pretty as lilies are, the whole house now smells like cat's piss, you can't shift that stench for love nor money. Hang on! Why did he buy me flowers?

Purchasing flowers did not get Joe out off shopping tonight, and as we stood in the queue at the checkout I remarked to Joe how I'd noticed there are a lot of men with one long fingernail, usually the pinky. Was this some sort of members-only sign like in the Masons? He laughed and followed it with 'It's for picking their nose.' I immediately demanded that Joe showed me both his hands, satisfied he didn't have a 'bogey nail'. I shot the cashier guy a look like he was vermin as he did possess one.

Joe, jack of all trades, doer of *none* – not in this house, anyway. Three weeks I've been waiting for the shelves in the kitchen to be put up, so I did it myself. He comes home and starts pointing out they're wonky. Whatever. At least they're up. He continued to nitpick, asks me what screwdriver I used, as he knows his tools are all locked away. Stupid question, the tool for all jobs: a butter knife, of course.

It was only two shelves but I guarantee if Joe had done it there would have been fourteen different tools, definitely a spirit level, the re-measuring of the same thing over and over again, several cups of tea, just as many fag breaks, a minimum three starts, six pauses, seven step-backs, and completion by tomorrow.

Wednesday 22nd February 2014

Tony and Leigh school disco 7.30pm.

Elizabeth's done something very surprising. Whilst concentrating on her pelvic floor thrust, Rico kissed her. Shocked and stunned she told him no, but that was after she'd been kissing him back for ten minutes. Reckons she should feel dirty and ashamed, and yet is so looking forward to next week, hoping he'll do more than kiss her. Not sure if the idea of adultery bothers her more than the idea that she's no better than Julie, lmao.

Tony and Leigh have their school disco tonight. Oh, the school disco: 'Truly 'by Lionel Ritchie, 'You Make Me Feel Brand New', The Stylistics. Dancing with your hands on each other's waists, too shy to get any closer unless you were already a couple, then it was arms around the neck every dark corner had someone snogging in it, usually Julie, lol. Alcohol was sneaked into the punch, inevitable fights, girls being dumped for the one who put out. Dear oh dear, Julie has a lot to answer for, lol. xx

Thursday 23rd February 2014

Elizabeth arrives London.

Chloe arrives London.

Tony and Leigh dentist 5pm.

Elizabeth called to say she'd arrived at her sister Jemima's and should be here by four tomorrow, then we'll hit Mickey's around seven with a vengeance.80s night, luv it.

All's well at Tony and Leigh's dental check-up. Leigh made a good point: why do dentists have bad breath and tons of fillings? Maybe that's why they got involved in dentistry! This goes with the question about rock stars: when they debut they already have the signature long hair, suited to their genre, but it aint grown overnight I'm sure; so do they not even attempt to break into the music industry until the hair is the right length? Can't be coincidence, can it?

Saturday 25th February 2014

Leg wax 2pm.

Elizabeth was the first to arrive at mine yesterday, with freshly printed 'Choose Life' T-shirts, so matched with our shorts and white boots we hit the town.80s night, the usual club segregation, like the setting of *Seven Brides for Seven Brothers*:

on the left with frilly shirts and espadrilles, Duran Duranies; on the cool right, Wham'ettes. The only thing we all ever agree on is given five minutes alone with George Michael we could convert him. Great night! Chloe won a free bottle of champagne for best impersonation: Tina Turner, no less. What the judge didn't realise was she hadn't perfected Miss Turner's walk, it was the shoes she was wearing having lived in her wellies since the move her feet were banging in the heels. Still, free booze is not to be sniffed at. We bumped into Jenny Higgins, she was the head girl at school, still as smug as ever but definitely packing a little more junk in the trunk, lol. Clearly in denial as she flounced about telling all and sundry she's still a size 10, right up to the moment her 5 inch heel touched the very polished dance floor and she stacked it, her mini skirt ripped, and hanging open exposing her massive arse, pml. There is a God! xx

Julie, as predicted, (lived in hope she wouldn't) at the mere intro of Michael Jackson began her robotic moves, propelling me back 25 years to the exact feeling of mortification. Chloe left bright and early, looking as rough as shark shit and still limping. Elizabeth has gone back to Jemima's.

Leg wax at 2pm. The pain will not be enough to distract me from the joyous memory of Higgins going arse over tit.

Think I'll have an early night; feeling a bit funny.

Sunday 26th February 2014

Dinner at Andy and Jess's.

I'm still feeling little bit dodgy from the tequila slammers. Seriously, how old am I? xx

Going round Andy and Jessica's for dinner; God, I hope I don't throw up.

Elizabeth texted me to say she'd arrived safely back in the Big Apple.

I managed to eat without razzing round Andy's and Jessica's then had an instant recovery when Julie rang to tell me that when the alarms in Mickey's had been tripped at four this morning, the police arrived to find Jenny Higgins wandering around, having been locked in after passing out in the toilet, because she'd drunk herself into a stupor from shaming face plant. They held her at the station for three hours until she'd convinced them she wasn't casing the joint. I'm growing more and more religious every day: thank you, Lord.

Monday 27th February 2014

Joe football.

Shopping.

Went for a potter in town and remembered there was a jacket I liked in Dolly Birds, but wasn't prepared to pay £175 for it, so given that they were having a sale I hoped it would be there, so in I went. Interestingly it was in the sale, except the price tag now said 'Was £225, Now Only £199'! Now I'm no grade A mathematician but that aint right, if indeed legal, is it? Clever though. Almost as clever as the other scam we sussed several years ago. The most popular shop on the High Street neither sells great quality nor the most attractive clothing and is ridiculously expensive, yet a lot of women keep on going there. Me and Julie never gain any weight so I can buy an 8 from any shop or market stall and it fits; likewise with Julie's size 10, yet an 8 from this particular shop falls off me. Literally. Clever, eh! Bigger birds can fit into smaller sizes, makes them feel better and they can show disbelieving friends the tag, proving they're not as 'big' as some have bitched.

Met Julie for coffee and decided we'd have it sat in the park. We were soon joined by the tramps hoping to cadge a fiver. Julie can't stand scroungers so politely said, 'Piss off, mate.' This triggered the smaller of the bunch to shout at the one who was scrounging that he'd offended the lady. Lady? Ooh, funny. Scrounger retaliated, and the next minute they're having a full on punch-up. They fell on Julie, she starts heaving at the stench then she gets one bloke in a headlock. As I step in to help she swings her right fist, misses Stinky and smacks me in the mouth. I swear you cannot buy this shit, we laughed for a good half an hour before she insisted we had to get home and burn our clothing.

Using the sympathy card of my split lip I tried to con Joe out of the cash for a new settee. Got some old codswallop about the suite being only two years old! That man is tighter than a camel's arse in a sandstorm, makes me sick!

Wednesday 29th February 2014

Hairdresser 5pm.

Window cleaner.

So far all Elizabeth has done is stole the odd kiss, but has now decided she wants this man. The penny has finally dropped and she now knows what Veronica and Matilda were hinting at with the exchange of glances, claiming to be not so stupid as to think this attention is only aimed at her, and says she can play nicely and share. Is promiscuous catching?

Julie is calling Liz tonight; this should be interesting if

Elizabeth tells her what she's been up to. If it was me I wouldn't say nowt. *Never* give Julie petrol for the fire.

Chloe and Elizabeth will be arriving here around 2pm having roped them in for the France trip on Saturday. Girls' night at Tina's tomorrow, should really cancel as we've gotta be at the coach stop for 4am Saturday, lol. So not gonna happen. xx

Had a great idea for the parents that don't wanna pay child maintenance; well, they do, but don't trust the ex will spend it on the kids and not themselves. Why don't the government set up something like a catalogue system that maintenance goes into an account and the parent with the custody can order items needed, like clothing, beds, etc. Genius.

France trip leaves 4am.

As guessed we did have girls' night at Tina's as planned. We unanimously decided we'd stay up all night, so I am knackered, but I shall sleep like a baby now. Who'd have thought an ordinary day in France could bring such joy? Or maybe I need to get a life? having had to grit my teeth when Jenny Higgins had boarded the coach, believing the trip was gonna be hell, I was rewarded thrice-fold when upon arrival in Paris, Jenny rushed to the loo and came out declaring in her snotty belittling tone how the French have weird hand basins. myself having been to

France on several occasions could feel the demonic smile spread across my face as I had the greatest pleasure telling her that the toilets were unisex and that she had in fact washed her hands in the gents' urinal. I almost pitied her as she begged me to keep this between ourselves. Yeah, right. xx

Monday 5th March 2014

Joe football.

Shopping.

It's Monday! or as it's now known, Doctor Day. Chris has had two nosebleeds over the weekend so I'm guessing she was the first through the surgery doors this morning. She gets here at nine to tell me the doc has ruled out haemophilia as the blood clearly clotted, and has reluctantly taken blood to test for leukaemia which was Chris's second choice, lol.

Kids nowadays are brainy but have not a scrap of common sense: Tony's mate argued vehemently with me that prawns were a vegetable, chicken is not meat, To think these are the people who will be caring for us one day.

Tuesday 6th March 2014

Pancake Day.

One burnt frying pan,2pound of sugar in carpet, and two grease spots on ceiling - not bad, considering Joe was involved.

Wednesday 7th March 2014

Taking grandkids shopping.

Chloe and Liz arriving 2pm.

It's Tina's 40thbirthday tomorrow: she's out having dinner with Mark, the rest of us are over Caroline's who is having an Ann Summers party. Friday we're all at Manero's club and Saturday Mark's throwing her a party at Rifles which all couples are going to. Probably be dead by Sunday, lol.

Sunday 11th March 2014

I'm no prude but it amazes me that in the right situation a female will not only admit to having one, but will report on the performance and durability of their sex aids, like at these 'buying parties' as now they think they're in the company of fellow users. Er, *no*, truth be known, most of us are only there for a girls' piss-up with a few laughs. Even Caroline was a bit stunned when her neighbour told us how she's got one of everything, that her husband works away and she misses him. Fair enough, but on further questioning her sister said the husband is only ever away for one night at a time. Get a life, luv. Apart from how scary some of these gadgets look, one in particular resembled a neon cactus that vibrates spins and bends. The noise? Hardly discreet. Each to their own, for who am I to judge? But please, what's up with the birds who go shopping with things shoved in their drawers, or worse. How sad are you? What if they got hit by a bus? The shame in the Emergency Department. Sure I read somewhere that marriages can be destroyed as men take real offence to their women needing something other than them to get off on. Not for me, thanks.

Friday I'd made a start on the grandkids' costumes for Book Day: Sam wants to be Captain Hook; Connor, Tic Toc; and Daisy, Tinkerbell. No pressure then. Julie arrived at mine around seven, closely followed by the others, and we headed off to Manero's. This being Jenny Higgins's favourite haunt I was relieved but undeniable surprised to find she was missing; elation followed as her mate informed me that as Jenny was getting ready she'd been distracted by a mouse that had legged it out from under her bed while she had the curling tongs on her fringe, and she has literally burnt the *whole* fringe off. Mate, if laughing is a punishable sin I shall surely burn in hell. xx

Paul arrived at one on Saturday where he accompanied Joe and the guys at Flannigan's; all were under strict instructions not to come back bladdered as we had to be at rifles for 7.30 for Tina's party. The whole night was excellent and I live to tell the tale, unlike Joe who at this moment is unconscious on the sofa after spewing his ring up. Chloe and Paul slinked off to the station at nine this morning, decked out in sunglasses; Elizabeth and Arthur departed soon after, and Julie is still in Leigh's room trying to sleep off a bottle of Jack Daniels, lol

As for me, there's clearly no rest for the wicked so I'm running around after everyone else.

Monday 12th March 2014

Nan's birthday.

Popped in the supermarket to see Caroline this morning to be told that apparently gimp boy Jonathon had been busted for masturbating at the till as he served customers. He's new to the cashier position, having worked in the bakery, and was removed for masturbating in the store room next to the flour bags, lol. What did management think was gonna happen, or did they think it was the smell of bread that turned him on? Bet they don't sack him! Full name Jonathon *Higgins*, brother of said slapper, married to store manager.

Speaking of slappers, no Julie for a week: she's jetted off to Italy in Charles's private jet on business. She should marry him, Christ knows he's asked enough times. Let's face it, any man that accepts that girl with all her shortcomings is a great catch.

Joe still has got a hangover. I'm not convinced it's not just an excuse to get out of dinner at Mum's tonight for Nan's 77th birthday. Tough shit, he's going.

Wednesday 14th March 2014

Sandra's birthday.

Yesterday was a good day, having cashed in my belated Christmas present of one Indian head massage.

Tension was soon back this morning as Leigh reminded me I'd agreed to go shopping with her this morning. In fairness it was quite an easy trip, assisted by the fact there was nothing that caught her eye. I on the other hand have purchased more knickers. Why? I don't know. I need help.

Will be going to Sandra's around six tonight to drop off her birthday presents. Can't believe she's old enough to be Chloe's mum: at fifty-nine she looks more like forty-five. Bet she don't have bingos.

St Patrick's Day, Flannigan's 7.30pm.

We're all off to Flannigan's tonight; I probably won't be coherent for 48 hours, the Irish are bad enough when it's not St Patricks Day, lol.

Can hear squeaking again. I'll save that information for Joe until tomorrow, don't want to ruin his night out. Come to think of it there is a lot of mousy activity at the moment: first neighbour Mary- well, in fairness, that was tights – then there was Higgins and the fringe incident, lol. Oh, very lol.

Sean's 32nd birthday.

Friday's girls night was cancelled out of respect for Abigail as it was the 35th anniversary of her mum's death, bless her. Abigail was only nine when she died. I know I moan about my mum but for all her faults I'm lucky to have her.

Me and Joe decided we'd bugger off to the caravan Friday night. Andy, Jessica and the kids joined us on Saturday morning. We got back home about four o'clock today; I'd forgotten it was Joe's brother's birthday. Surprise surprise, they're going Flannigan's. Good luck boys, it's Sunday.

Like scissors, you can never find the nail clippers. Someone must know where they are cos how else is some disgusting creature able to leave clippings on the chair?

Julie home from Italy today, she should be here by six: gossip, dinner and wine. Good luck Debbie, it's Sunday.

Joe football.

We so learn a new thing every day, lol. Leigh had spent best part of last night at accident and emergency with Keera, having got a frantic call from Keera's boyfriend Craig that he'd broke his banjo masturbating! Had me intrigued. Had me in stitches when explained, aided by a poorly drawn picture, what a banjo was on a boy's anatomy. Gotta hurt.

Joe rolled in (literally) around two this morning, looked none to pretty when he left for work this morning. I gave him that look, held it long enough for him to leave, then I shoved the paracetomol down my throat, hoping to kill off the bass drummer in my head. Tenner says he has a miraculous recovery when it's time to go football tonight. Got to go shopping; Chris has just texted me and said she'll meet me outside doctors. Mate, just consume entire contents of the medicine cabinet, Debbie, and be done with it.

I have somehow survived the day. Joe as predicted has gone to football. Chris lives to fight another day, as the assumed tumour in her ear turned out to be no more than a blind spot. Called Chloe and she informed me that the new lambs are starting to be born; got strangely emotional. WTF?

Mutley vets 9am.

Dragged Mutley to vets for his monthly de-fleaing and worming as the caring owner that I am. He repays me by throwing up in the car. Took me an hour an half to clear it up, seventy minutes of it was me trying to actually build up the stomach to scrape it off the seat. Ten minutes later Jessica calls to say she's stuck in traffic and could I pick Daisy up from nursery. Lucky for her she sits on a booster seat or she'd have got a chapped arse. I could see her screwing her face up in my mirror so was guessing the smell was lingering. This face-pulling and the now fiddling with her lughole continued long after we got in the house, so one mused, 'Have you got a flea in ya ear?' She mumbles, 'Nah, it's a stone, Nanny.' Two hours later we were back from A&E with in fact two stones and two small leaves. Every village has one, but I fear we may have two.

Thursday 22nd March 2014

Doing a spot of gardening out the front earlier when in my peripheral vision I saw something blue fly past, followed by a loud bang. On the grass verge opposite a car was wrapped around a tree. Being the good citizen I am, I and several others raced over to find a very old little lady sitting in the driver's seat, whining she forgot which one was the brake. Other than shocked, she wasn't injured in the slightest. If she'd done that half an hour later she'd have killed someone, as that's the place the little kids play after school. I walked away, quickly. Why are these old people still driving? Reflexes are shit. Eyesight is shit. Memory is shit. And yet the law says all they have to do is renew their licence when they're seventy; surely they should at least retake their tests to see if indeed we're not allowing a loaded gun to roam our roads.

I'm off to pack for Scotland tomorrow, although only a short stay. I have estimated at least 519 miles between me and Chris, as she'll be at the caravan with Abigail. Anything after that is a bonus.

Chloe's 41st birthday.

Me and Julie made it to the station on Friday by 5am; think she'd rolled out of Jeremy's bed around ten too. Four hours later we arrived to be met by Elizabeth decked out in Burberry. The farmhouse is amazing, had the tour and I was sold on the idea of moving. Chris texted me to see if I'd arrived safely, aww. Quickly followed up with do I have the number for the doctors in Sheppey, just in case. Unbelievable. We spent the evening in front of the huge open fire talking and drinking homebrew, courtesy of Mrs Shona Stroker, laughed ourselves silly when Chloe told us her husband is Willie. How we made it to town this morning for Chloe's birthday breakfast I do not know, it took everything I had to remember what my name was. That shit comes in jars, no labels, oh mate, excellent. We saw Elizabeth off at the airport and me and Julie arrived home here around five. Immediately I told Joe we should move to Scotland. He said he was more concerned about my reasons: was it the fresh air, the open country, or simply the moonshine? Er, hello, didn't like what he was insinuating.

Monday 26th March 2014

Spent yesterday putting the house back in order after my short absence. Chris is still away; it kind of messed up my Monday morning it's become habitual to lose an hour or so listening to her latest illness. I missed her. xx

That moment of madness quickly passed and I went shopping, bumped into Penny who was on her way to get a coffee after swimming ten lengths at the pool. Ten lengths! Why? Who would?

Most amusing when the local nutter arrived at the bakers: I'm guessing he was not very happy with the quality of his rolls, and to back up his claim that the soft rolls were hard, proceeded to bounce all five of them one by one off the manager's head.

Tuesday 27th March 2014

Chloe called to make sure we'd made a full recovery from 'no name in jam jar'; sadly I have. You'd never know with Julie, her brain's addled with or without alcohol. It seems Paul has decided not to shave anymore; Chloe's not feeling it, lol. When I told Julie later she was threatening to have Chloe admitted on the grounds of insanity, as Paul will now be rugged, rough and ready, very Clooney. Except Chloe reckons he's more Cat Weasel than George. Besides, I quickly reminded Julie that she likes her prey hairless. Shamelessly admitted she'd make an exception for Paul, and with Joe she'd take him anyhow.

Wednesday 28th March 2014

Hairdresser 5pm

Reality has hit me like a sledgehammer after spending ten minutes frantically searching for my glasses and realising I was already wearing them. I was now faced with 2 questions: (1) Am I going senile? (2)When the hell did I start wearing bloody glasses? Neither of which I have the answer to.

Window cleaner.

Joe came in from work asked me how my day was. Not unusual, except he did it in the guise of the Elephant Man including dribbling from the corner of his lips. He didn't laugh along with me, so that left me sure that Joe had had a stroke: his mouth wasn't moving right when he spoke and his speech was slurred. Was about to have a panic fit when he told me he has an ulcer. One bollocking and a glass of salt water later, he's a little better and I've returned the insurance policy to its strong box.

Chris got back from the caravan on Thursday. I'd successfully avoided her until I remembered we were all round Julie's on Friday. And yes, Chris had been to the docs whilst away: she got stung by a jellyfish, so I'll give her that one. Abigail had told her the best thing for it was to pee on it so she'd downed drawers and pee'd on the jellyfish. Penny was relating the story of the winter vomiting virus that strikes every December, affecting mainly office staff. Chris was on the edge of her chair fishing for symptoms, not realising that it's the bullshit illness that comes from office Christmas party binges. Tina's all packed and ready to set off for Belgium tomorrow with Terry; Elizabeth and Arthur headed off for Venice this morning, won't hear from her until the 4th when we all meet up at Chloe's. It's Arthur's treat for Mothers Day.

Kids are out, Joe's at poker, so I'm gonna have a soak, watch a film and have an early night.

Sunday 1st April 2014

Mothers Day.

Elizabeth gets Venice, Julie's sent Violet for a weekend of pampering, and me I get both sets of parents too cook for. Oh, and let's not forget Chris when she gets back from the Sunday market. Well, that's shit. xx

Chris arrived around 1pm after her usual jaunt to the Sunday market. Has bought herself the nastiest dress I've ever seen, don't know what she was thinking. Not happy with my response she turns to Joe for support, to which he responds 'It's as ugly as a box of arseholes'. Six bunches of flowers, a pair of diamond studs, pamper day voucher, chocolates and three handmade cards. Going to bed a little happier.

Tuesday 3rd April 2014

Spent yesterday cleaning and shopping as we're going to be leaving on Wednesday for Chloe and Paul's; nothing worse than going away and coming home to stuff, or is it that I am indeed, as Joe said, anal? Lol, rich coming from the man who still goes to football.

Tina and Terry got back from Belgium in just enough time for her to wash everything to repack it for Scotland, then of course there was Chris and it was a Monday: ohh. She had a mole that fell off. Only she would know if the body was missing one.

Spoke to Chloe; Liz and Arthur are already there, having flown straight from Venice. Should be a good time. The party is to celebrate eighteen years of happy marriage, lol. Is it? Or just the best excuse for more 'in a jar with no name'. xx

Mum's 61st birthday.

Train journey to Scotland on Wednesday was a blast: me, Joe, Chris and the kids, Tina, Terry, Julie and Charles. Chris twisted her ankle as she jumped on the train trying to avoid 'the gap'. We arrived at Chloe's pleased to find that Paul did not look like grizzly Adams. If he had, we wouldn't have noticed as all eyes fell on Liz, who was sporting some backcombed monstrosity on her head. 'Very chic to tease. 'Tease? Tortured, more like.

We had lunch and took the kids to the town to buy some last-minute party stuff. Paul took the guys to the local; they were all invited to go shooting on Angus Farley's farm. Joe reckons he's a master shooter. Hmm, probably got something to do with genes as he had two uncles that did bird for armed robbery.

Thursday we partied together to the early hours and left around six this morning. Elizabeth and Arthur took Baby and Molly with them to the airport as the girls were going from Scotland to their dads. The train journey back wasn't as much fun as going: tired, hung-over and trapped in a carriage with Chris still whining about her ankle – the same ankle that didn't stop her chasing the lambs around the barn with the kids.

Texted Mum when we got in to wish her Happy Birthday. Her and Dad are away so we're having them for dinner on Sunday as a belated gift.

It's now 3.15am Saturday morning. I've been woken up by a text message from Elizabeth. 'What on earth is a chav?' Apparently my reply of 'a pleb' did not suffice, and as she was not gonna drop it I've had to email her a more literate version: a chav is 'a sub-cultural stereotype' fixated on fashions usually consisting of Reebok classics, McKenzie polo shirts and a baseball cap – Burberry is their god. Bling in the earlobe, favoured music: rap rave and R&B. Who wrote this? And what have you done with me? This has come about because the *New York Times* has run a story on 'the delinquent youth' in England. That's rich considering their youth's gun-toting activities. Americans are a bit outdated as this fad has passed here; maybe that's where they all went, lol.

Joanna's boy went through this phase; she admits it was amusing at the beginning, even reminded her of us at school – that became her downfall. Beginning stages of transformation, an amateur Chav spends a lot of time on its appearance: cleanliness and toiletries vital, excessive use of expensive aftershave even though they've only got bum fluff on the chin. This stage is welcomed with open arms as only a few months ago the same kid was known as the soap dodger. Then comes the cap, you'd be wrong to think this just pops onto the head: oh no, it requires precision, it has to sit balanced upwards on the back of the head. Joanna said at this stage it was normal to come home from work and find a dozen of them in her house; she would know they were there as she could smell the aftershave before she even got her key in the door. On several occasions I was round hers the chavs were always well-mannered, polite and respectful, but mostly funny: I'd never heard so much bullshit fall freely out of anyone's mouth.

This is where Joanna's youth bit her in the arse, having relayed to them the tales of our youth, they had quickly realised that she was clearly a chavette in her teens: this gave her 'legend' status in their eyes. This is where the alarm bells should have rung, but ego is a bastard, she took it as a innocent fad and before she knew it her boy had switched from smart and clean to scruffy and sneaky, the cap was replaced by the hoody, the familiar faces he used to call mates had all vanished and been replaced with others. You'd be met by silence if you dare ask 'Who's he?' These are new faces – if, in fact, you can even see into their hoody that is – no more 'Hi Jo', the only response she got on greeting was a nod or a suspicious glare.

So where she had once welcomed the vibrancy of youth into her home she began telling Terry that no one was allowed into her house. She began doing weekly stock checks on personal possessions. This wasn't a case of a parent moaning about fashion, including hating seeing the boxer shorts with the jeans below the arse, it's about watching someone you love turning into a stranger, worrying the hell out of you that every time they get a text or have a mumbled conversation on the mobile they whip out the front door, your heart races every time you hear a siren, crime and drugs are at the forefront of your mind. We may give birth to these kids but that don't make them perfect, as we'd like to believe. These things do go on in our society and unlike we'd like to believe, it's not always someone else's kids that are the problem ones. She had several confrontations with Terry, he was in denial about his new persona and told Joanna she was paranoid. Paranoia is a personality disorder characterised by a mistrust of others and a constant suspicion that people around you have a sinister motives, excessive trust in their own knowledge and abilities, and avoiding close relationships. They search for hidden meaning in everything and read hostile intentions into the actions of others, they are quick to challenge the loyalty of friends and loved ones, often appearing cold and distant. They usually shift blame to others, also tend to carry long grudges. Who's really paranoid?

The magic of motherhood, we give birth and it's instantaneous love. Protective to the point you'd die or even kill for them, the realism is motherhood is flawed, it has no cut-off point. When our skills are no longer welcomed we are seen as interfering and an hindrance, and in truth you'd rather not have an emotional attachment anymore because the worry and stress is slowly killing you.

Terry was the first thing on her mind when she woke up and the last when she went to bed, ifs and buts: does he look thin and drawn because he's playing football with his mates at all hours, or is it drug abuse? Is the abundance of jewellery she bought him down to a few items because it is in his room, or has he had to sell it? She can't look herself, access to his room was stopped; she daren't ask who was on the phone, was never be privy to what's being exchanged on Facebook as the page was immediately closed as she entered the room. His appearance made him look like a vagrant, and uncomfortable. He doesn't walk like a human, now he bowls along like a Neanderthal. Every word that leaves his mouth - albeit few - are derogatory, negative, acting like the world and everyone in it owes him something.

Jo watched her son turn into a stranger, and I watched her go from an hardworking, confident, independent woman to a near nervous recluse. She blames herself; this was never her doing, but as the parent the finger of blame has fallen on her. What is she guilty of? Loving the boy, nursing him through illness? We should all heed these warning signs. Unless we lock them away till they're thirty then any of ours are as vulnerable as the rest.

If it's a female Chav, other than the appearance they fit the same criteria as their male counterpart, only they come with the added bonus of coming home pregnant because - scarily - most are sexually active at fourteen. As for Terry, he is in prison for car theft and dealing to minors. Why on earth am I having this conversation?

I'm going back to bed, it's hurt my head.

Saturday 7th April 2014

Leg wax 2pm.

After this morning's rant I have pondered further the argument that parents are not to blame, and have to say in fairness some parents are shit, like the young mum I saw in a documentary: what chance did her three have? She was on drugs all through her pregnancy, she supplies her kids with drugs; apparently this is better than them going to a backstreet dealer, in her head she believes she is doing the right thing.

Although I'm 100% anti-drugs myself, when Aunt Dina was diagnosed terminal she began smoking cannabis between her doses of pain relief and even I had to turn the other cheek. I may be a law-abiding citizen but I'm no bleeding martyr.

Sunday 8th April 2014

Mum and Dad dinner 3pm.

I am so tired, struggled to cook dinner earlier. I could have happily curled up and gone to sleep. I think I'll go to doctor's tomorrow.

Monday 9th April 2014

Hypochondriacs is why none of us can get into see a doctor on a Monday morning, we have to wait two weeks for an appointment. And God forbid you need treatment on a Friday, you've got bob hope and no hope as they'll be there panicking about the weekend because the docs are closed Saturday and Sunday. Seriously, Chris!

Joe bailed on football and stayed in with me as I was once again laying on the sofa knackered. Aww, I love that guy.

Tuesday 10th April 2014

Terry's 43rd birthday.

In contrast to yesterday I have been up early with boundless energy and so decided to spring clean. Actually, 'decided' is not accurate: it's a primal urge. So out came the old music, up went the volume, and the madness began. The house is sparkling and I'm £3.72 richer after delving in the creases of the sofa, ha ha, finders rights. Not a stone unturned, not a curtain unwashed. Nan always says the state of your curtains tells the outside the state of the inside of your home. I do all this around six times a year, so why is it called spring clean? Then again, I am anal, lol. xx

Chloe has flown out to Los Angeles to see Jeni and Jaki, Julie's in Greece, Joe and the others are all at Flannigan's for Terry's birthday,

I dare him to come home and puke anywhere in my lovely clean house.

Wednesday 11th April 2014

I must have looked in the bathroom mirror a hundred times, yet this morning I 'really looked'. I was shocked, I won't lie. When the hell did I start collecting wrinkles? Stab in the dark here, but I'm thinking it was probably before I got fucking glasses, whenever that was. First thought, 'Who the hell is that old bird?' Like a classic horror movie when someone stands in front of the mirror and standing behind them appears the face from hell. Second issue: only one face in the mirror and it was mine. What the hell happened? Last time I looked I was doing OK. When was that? Shit, 1985.

Back from shops armed with face creams.

Friday 13th April 2014

Margaret's 67th birthday.

Yesterday was dull; well, except for the new conifer man.

We're taking Joe's parents for lunch today for his mum's birthday, accompanied by the brothers and their wives. Chris has rung me four times already and it's only ten o'clock: the girls are travelling back from their dad's today and Mum has stupidly reminded her it's again Friday 13th. Notice Mum's switched her mobile off: how convenient, luv. Marie is picking them up from the airport. Their dad used to get a limo to do it but too many questions got asked in Chris's street. Girls' night tonight. Julie's still in Greece, so thankfully Tina will be there otherwise I'd be stuck with Abigail, Penny and Chris all sharing the one brain cell.

Saturday 14th April 2014

Aunt Shirley 55th birthday.

Aunt Shirley has moved back over here from Australia, staying with Mum at the moment, and as it's her birthday, me, Mum and Chris all had lunch and went shopping with her. Had a great afternoon then somewhere between six and seven I had a mental breakdown.

As it seems the 'so not true I'm having a MLC' has once more robbed me of my dignity, when this evening I flounced into the front room stating in a firm almost aggressive voice, 'I need to go clubbing, I need to dance and sing', with a pointed finger in Joe's face, 'Don't bother trying to stop me!' followed with, 'I've selflessly given my life to you, so understand, shut up and put up, luv.' Was doing OK until he slipped in, 'You already do, you've never given up your girls' nights out?' In desperation I did what any self-respecting woman who had just made a complete arse of herself would do, and yelled, 'Yeah, well, as long as we're clear on that!' Then stormed out. It took all my resolve not to run back in and punch him when I heard him snickering.

Note to self: Must fix connection between brain and mouth. Secondly: WTF?

Monday 16th April 2014

Academic Tutor Day9am.

Just got back from Academic Tutor Day. Nice to see teachers have finally got trendier, they don't call it Parents Evening any more. Is that because it's held during the day now, or because a lot of kids only have one parent? Like the modernisation of the name the teachers definitely appeared younger and trendier, the kids seem to have a real rapport with them which seems to have the knock-on effect of the pupils interacting with them on friendly terms and a willingness to work hard in lessons. Not like in my day: Sirs wore baggy cord trousers, cotton shirt, blazer and brogues, all un-ironed and never matching; for Miss it was flowing skirts or frock with a misshapen cardigan, hideous shoes, and in summer she would wear men's sandals. I remember how shocked we were when they told us their real ages: most were in their thirties but they all looked around fifty.

10.05 on the dot and here she was, Chris. Oh, how she hasn't been barred from the surgery I do not know. She tells me she had a stabbing pain in her boob since yesterday, she'd been shopping, bought herself a large seeded crusty loaf, filled it with cheese, did some ironing. All was well, then the pain began. She glanced down her top and saw black dots around her nipple, and having read somewhere that if the nipple changes appearance you should seek medical examination immediately, this morning on further examination the doctor with a flick of a nail removed three poppy seeds that had fallen from her sandwich the day before. Mate, hope he don't think we're all like her.

Tuesday 17th April 2014

Tina and Terry's anniversary. They're going to dinner and to see *Les Miserable's*. My *les miserable* will be home around five, lol.

One thing that really pisses me off: I and many I know have always owned dogs and never leave poop when we go out. I've even been known to go home and get bucket of water and disinfectant when Mutley had a dose of trots. Many of these culprits think that walking the dog around of the edge of the local playing field till it craps is OK, and in the same breath moan when their kids play on the same field and come home with it on their clothes.

Wednesday 18th April 2014

Joe's fed up that every time he pulls up to the drive Mrs Davis is spying on him from behind the drapes, lol. We're all quick to have a pop about these people, but curtain shufflers are better than guard dogs: definitely have less burglaries in your street if you have one.

Chloe's home safe and sound from Los Angeles.

Doctors blood test 9am.

Got thrush!

Nasty. You only have to have this pleasure once and that's enough for any mere mortal. Called Elizabeth; she thought I'd rescued a songbird. Songbird? More like fucking termites. I'm not keen on medicines and the like, I would rather suffer than pump my body full of chemicals, but at the first inkling of thrush last night I rushed so fast to the bathroom to my stash of fungal cream I had smoke coming off my heels. There are two reasons any person would have a stash.(1)If you've had thrush before, then no explanation required.(2)Less trips to the chemist where you encounter the woman that works the counter who really gets up your nose: 'Have you had thrush before?'- patronising tone -'If you've had thrush more than twice in a year, you should consult a doctor. 'You'll need a doctor if you don't hand over that box, luv. Good God, unless they're selling adult scratch mitts or a coconut doormat So's I can sit and wiggle on it, I'll take my chances with the pessary, thank you.

Elizabeth, not grasping the conversation whilst talking to me on the phone, made the mistake of texting Julie, wanting to know what the chemist has got to do with a bird. Julie bluntly replied that thrush is a fungal infection of the Minge, lol. I can't believe Liz has never experienced it, let alone never heard of it. She wanted to know what signs she should look for.

Hmm, it begins with the first itch (the lone termite) and with it comes an angel on your left shoulder, on your right comes Satan, good versus evil. Calmly and sensibly the voice of reason tells you, 'Don't scratch, you'll only make it worse, you'll be sorry.' While Satan whispers, 'Go on, one little scratch, think of the relief. 'By now you'll be struggling, seeking some relief. You think, 'Go for a wee.' Arhh, the stingy flow of water, soothing, but oh! Drip dry or wipe? Even your angel of conscience knows that drip drying could bring more problems, so with an inner smugness Satan pipes up with a compromise, 'Don't wipe, just dab.' Every bloody time you'll fall for it. Within seconds of the toilet paper touching your crotch you release the colony of termites and have rubbed so hard the tissue is now the consistency of talc and your Minge looks like a cocoa bean, or as Julie once said, 'Your nets are showing through the drapes.'

On the plus side thrush is the best deterrent for amorous advances from hubby: don't bother with the 'I've got a headache', just tell him you think you've got thrush and he'll turn over so fast he'll leave a vapour trail. Unless he's never experienced this delight, then humour him and I guarantee the memory will imbed itself in his libido for all eternity. Elizabeth's response not a shock: 'You really are quite disgusting.'

Blood test done.

Good Friday tomorrow so we're off to the caravan for the day.

Positives: Fungal cream packed.

Saturday 21st April 2014

Were babysitting tonight so we thought it would be a good idea to let the kids burn off some energy at the park, so we stopped off at the shop to buy stuff to feed the squirrels. When I was reading the writing on the packet of monkey nuts I laughed to see, 'May contain traces of nuts'! I should bloody hope so. Saying that, there are some who aint too clued up. Joe's sister, on accepting an invitation to dinner, was offered trifle with a nutty topping and politely explained to her host that she is allergic to nuts so would decline the dessert. She was offered the alternative, a slice of coconut cake, again offer was declined. Immediately the host, after pondering what she could offer as a substitute, declared, 'Ooh, what about an almond slice?' Der the clue is in the title, people. Why on earth would anyone with this dangerous allergy ever consider eating out? However, this may explain why when they do, and have informed the restaurant manager they can't have nuts, they still end up leaving the establishment in an ambulance.

Gotta go shopping for BBQ tomorrow and add finishing touches for the Easter Egg Hunt.

Monday 23rd April 2014

Yesterdays BBQ and Easter Egg Hunt was good fun. Charles, bless him, was dragged around holding Daisy's basket as she rummaged and stole eggs from the boys' baskets when they weren't looking. Julie was more competitive than the kids and wrestled with Connor twice for the same egg. Rhianne managed to gather two eggs as she was afraid of everything from snails to leaves. Was overjoyed when Chloe and Paul turned up. Whole day was excellent, only one child sick through chocolate overdose, several bruises and Terry chipped a tooth wheelbarrow racing. Still, what did he expect with Joe holding his legs, lol? Got off light, if you ask me. Chloe and Paul left about eleven this morning and have headed off for her mum's, then home. I've put the house and garden back in order, haven't cleaned the BBQ: think I'll leave that for Joe. He's got football later; don't blame him for going on a bank holiday, the only thing that'll be on TV is one of the many James Bond films. So with the telly well and truly off I shall enjoy the peace.

Last night's peace was interrupted, as a delicate matter has arisen. Elizabeth informed us all (via Facebook) that dear Arthur has been for a fitting for a toupee, and as her oldest and dearest friends she is relying on us to be understanding. Julie begged Liz to say she was lying as she was in fear of wetting her drawers. I would like to say me and Chloe were more supportive but we caved in long before Julie.

Note to self: Look up the meaning of 'friend'.

Apparently it's the done thing amongst the partners, they all have one, and Arthur has had the subtle suggestion to follow suit. Poor Arthur is just typically bald – hair round the sides, nowt on top – it's never bothered him, he never stood out from the crowd because he was bald. According to Elizabeth he may be viewed that he may be past his time. How shallow? I told her if he gets a rug, he is gonna draw attention to himself alright, mostly bad. I pass bald men in the street without giving them a second glance, but one dodgy brush-over or a syrup and I'm on it in a flash. I told her to set the shavers on 2, run it over his head: it'll not only knock years off him, at the same time giving him a rugged edge over his colleagues, more importantly it will ensure he's not ridiculed or stared at.

Chloe mentioned that it's rumoured that men with wigs are usually sad, immature individuals. This the words of a professional therapist, not Chloe stooping to the lowest form of friend. That's Julie's job. xx

So professional opinion describes these men as lecherous, believing that women who stare back at their leering faces do so because they find them and their hair irresistible. Quite sad, really: should we be mocking them? Yes we should, if this is about virility: 'I am man, hear me roar. 'Why, then, is it only middle-aged-plus doing it? Surely the younger balding guy would be too? The thing with toupees is they are placed on the head, blending in with nothing. They appear to come in limited colours: red, brown, salt 'n pepper. Never seen a black one, that shade seems to come in aerosol form which they spray over the patch and hope they don't sweat. It would help if these blokes actually went for the closest match to their own hair colour, but it's always red on grey, grey on brown, or salt 'n pepper on either.

Reminds me of the time me and Chloe were in the bakers having coffee when a customer approached the counter (obvious rug balanced on nupper) and the assistant asked if he'd like a saucer of milk. The look of bewilderment on his face had me in hysterics: he didn't have a clue. But I guess you have to be oblivious to go out like that.

Wednesday 25th April 2014

Hairdresser 5pm.

The last conversation I wanted was about hair loss. Still reflecting on Elizabeth's dilemma, I wanna know how these men introduce the hair piece for the first time. Do they call a family conference? If so, how come nobody stopped them? Or do they just come down to dinner one evening wearing it, and the family is so stunned they pretend not to have noticed they have road kill on their head? I love Dad dearly, but I can tell you either myself or Chris would have torn the critter from his head, pissing ourselves with laughter, and told him to get a grip. He'd never have got as far as the front door, let alone the street. Begs another question: are the women married to these men looking for revenge? They must be vindictive; I, like many loving wives, wouldn't let my man out in a creased shirt let alone looking like a twat!

Note to self: Ring and tell Arthur wig wearing has to be one of the highest forms of embarrassment you can reap onto the ones you love: *don't do it.*

Thursday 26th April 2014

Chloe arrives London.

Elizabeth arrives London.

Girl's night here.

Julie saw Tessie in BHS lingerie department on Tuesday, sizing up the thongs. Julie, being the perfect 10, cannot fathom why on earth big women would wear one. Clarifying that: 'big' as in 34-plus. Julie reckons the reason we women wear thongs is for either sexual reasons (Julie's mindset) or the obvious: making your arse look good in trousers, no knicker lines and emphasises of the cheeks, lol. Not meaning to sound rotten (she blatantly was)said if you have a really big rear end:

(1) you don't wanna draw attention to it,
(2) it's not going to make your arse seem better-shaped in clothes.

Elizabeth has confessed to never owning one as they seem a bit unhygienic. Julie subtle as ever - not - narked, 'Bet the Embryo does.' Elizabeth, out of character, retorted with, 'I'm sure the only reason you wear any drawers at all is for the purpose of keeping your ankles warm.' Ooh!

Jules, mate, credit where it's due: you got proper owned, lol. xx

Off to the shack tomorrow.

Within ten minutes of arriving at 'the shack' last night, another interesting point was raised! Following the thong debate, several glasses of wine and an apology from Elizabeth and Julie, we got onto push-up bras DD-plus! Why on earth would a woman with enormous breasts want to push them up? For the ones with small boobs, pushing them up would be OK, but the bras push them together as well, giving the illusion of having just one boob sitting in the middle of your chest, known in our circles as 'mono tit'.

Round Two of digs came as Julie stated, 'That's cos small-boobed women forget the vital ingredient, chicken fillets.' Carefully explaining to Liz in a clear and audible tone – making Liz look like a right div – that you don't eat them but stuff them in your bra. Unimpressed, Liz reckoned that to be more unhygienic than wearing underwear in butt crease. Julie was again stunned that she then had to explain they're not real chicken, but silicon. Which begged the question from all of us: where has Elizabeth been for the last 20 years? Elizabeth eventually caught up and made an interesting comment, that surely if a guy is drawn to your boobs and he ends up back at your place, wouldn't he be disappointed when he discovers half the goods stayed in the bra? All eyes fell on Julie. The font of all slut wisdom said, 'Nah, I should think by the time he discovers the truth he'll be gagging for it and won't give a toss.' Not so sure that this would apply to the guy who has pulled with the large trouser bulge which is actually rolled-up socks. Elizabeth tried to claw back some dignity for her serious lack of intelligence, playing the delayed jet-lag card. If only, bless her. Have a feeling the reason Elizabeth was so touchy about the topics is cos she herself is a bant (big arse, no tits), lol.

Medical emergency last night: after we all left the shack,

Julie met up with her casual flame, things got a bit heated and rushed, leading to poor Jeremy snagging his collar in his flies. Julie reckons she's never seen the colour drain from a face so fast.

Ooh, I have, when Joe got last month's credit card statement through, lol. xx

Monday 30th April 2014

Is hairspray flammable? Hell, yeah! We popped out to the Old Piper last night and saw some woman, two sheets to the wind, light her fag which ignited her fringe, in seconds engulfing her entire head. Yeah, it was funny! Apart from the horrendous smell that follows singed hair, she wasn't harmed.

What was that advert? Is she or isn't she wearing hairspray? Who were they trying to kid: if you can't see someone's wearing it then they haven't got enough on to do jack for the hair. To hold a style in place you have to cake it on, and you will now have a polyester look that does *not* blow naturally in the wind, and God forbid you get caught in the rain. 'So gentle you can run your fingers through it': go on try it, I dare you; it's gonna snag like a bitch. 'Brushes out', *not*: you'll be soaking it in conditioner and will have to give it a minimum three washes before all trace of it has gone. I could be wrong, but aren't these the same women who think red lipstick is cool? This should only be worn by a select few, or at least women with names like Porsche or Crystal. Not many people can carry it off, but many think they can. Still, the rest of us would have nothing to stare at when the lights go up in the clubs.

Charity shops: not a place I would be seen dead in. 'What a snobby attitude': lol, oh let's face it, it comes with a stigma and a *smell*. Grannies always say it's mothballs: whatever! It means if you can smell that on someone then you know where they shop. I've only bought something once from there, and it weren't clothes. I'd fancied doing a jigsaw with a ridiculous amount of pieces, went to the toy shop and they wanted £25, and someone suggested I look in the charity. Against my will I went and got four jigsaws for a fiver: bargain. And that's the point of these shops: they make money from donated goods and we get a bargain to boot. Apparently not. Sally, who has worked there for six years having been ousted to make room for the manageress's niece has blown the cover on what goes on in these so-called goodwill premises. It seems that these unpaid employees rummage through the bags and boxes first, not only taking for themselves but also for resale elsewhere, car boots and the like. What's left has a high mark-up, and the difference gets split between them all at closing time. Tut tut, thieving bastards. But then again, look at the majority of the women who work there: bad perms that match their bad attitudes, as most suspect are sex-starved spinsters or angry widows. Sally has labelled them rude, obnoxious, and up their own arses – not charitable. The genuine charitable volunteers, the good guys, appear at hospitals and fetes. These give their time to help, and won't be hard to spot as they're the ones who actually smile at you as you approach. Sally made the front page of the local *Guardian* with her saddened innocent face, lol. How many other readers are gonna notice she only blew the whistle after being pushed out? She'd been there six years and never said a word before. Busted, luv.

Note to self: Stay away from charity shops.

Wednesday 2nd May 2014

Chris had lunch with Abigail yesterday, said something about Abigail meeting a guy called Virgil at the poetry afternoon in the library. Says it all, really.

Thursday 3rd May 2014

Went round Chris's for dinner. I was fishing for dirt on this Virgil guy: how sad has my life got? Not looking good for him in my eyes as apparently today they went hiking in the hills. Jackie makes a surprise entrance and tells us she's pregnant. Chris was beside herself at the thought of being a grandmother. I was smiling for her until she states, 'And you'll be a great aunt!'Er, *no*. Drop the '*great*', that aint happening.

Friday 4th May 2014

Zero's 8pm.
    We've put a man on the moon, have we not? Then how come we can't program automatic doors to open and shut consistently? Darby's department store is notorious for it, as I experienced today, and so have many others I'm sure, As you approach you find yourself stalling, wondering if it's gonna open, or are you gonna crash face first into glass, making a right plum of yourself, or passing through will it try to shut with you in it, triggering alarms. So either way, all and sundry stare with amusement.

Paranoia tempts me to believe maybe there's nothing wrong with the technology and the truth, as some have suspected in the past, is that the doors are being controlled by someone inside the building who is doing it on purpose for their own fun, tweaking the controls, shall we say. I don't mind this so much; at least, if it was made aware to the public, we could play along for a prize.

Going Zero's tonight. To celebrate baby news.

Saturday 5th May 2014

Whilst clubbing at Zero's last night I met Abigail's new man, Virgil. God knows what she was wearing: she looked like a sixties throwback with her long floral frock and sandals. I didn't warm to him: looked like a train spotter and smelt like lentils. Worse than Abigail's 'Ooh, I'm an extra from *The Partridge Family*' look was the fact she had hairy armpits. I'm praying she was in a rush and forgot to shave; there was at least 48 hours worth of stubble. Very Continental, I'm sure but I personally wouldn't be seen dead looking like I'd shoved a Yorkshire terrier under each arm: fortnightly waxing will continue. Skanky bird. xx

I warmed to Virgil eventually. Definite sarcasm, lol. What a dick.

Got home and have realised that Virgil has grated on my psyche all night as I've chewed poor Joe's ears off that any man who encourages hair growth on a women is a cretin. But hey, what's it gotta do with me if someone wants to go all *au natural*? But what's next, though? Should we stop buying hair products, make-up, hair dye? Mate, I'd look like Cruella within a month, so that wouldn't be happening. Oh ha hee, laughing so much right now, *not* Don't like Virgil at all.

Sunday market.

Should have stayed in bed. Instead I made the mistake of going to the Sunday market with Chris where she managed to bore me to death in the cab on the way home with quotes from Virgil. It seems her and V got on like a house on fire: shocker there! He's convinced Chris that through our own vanity buying these products (knew it)are damaging our environment and wildlife. Might have known Chris would agree with him. I do agree that we shouldn't buy or encourage anything that's been tested on animals, especially for vanity, but there are many products available that haven't been squirted into bunnies' eyes, items such as deodorant are vital as people with niffy pits don't seem to notice they smell; it's the people around them that gag on their BO.

People like him always claim they're acting for the environment. Same as that woman I used to clean for in Chelsea: her famous line, 'I do my bit to save the planet', referring to the eco dolphin-friendly washing-up liquid, which sat alongside bleach, ant killing powder, fly spray aerosol form, slug pellets, rat poison and the friendly mouse trap that 'doesn't kill just entraps'. Begging the question: why does the mouse get better demise than the rat? Cos they're dense, maybe. People, not the rats: do they think that the cute little mouse doesn't cause the same problems in the house or with your health? Unlike fat ugly rat who's going to rub his plague-ridden body all over your surfaces, chew your wires, breed like mad and destroy anything of value just to nest?

Joe asked me what car does Virgil drove. I hadn't asked him, I had the impression that him and Abigail had arrived at the club on a pushbike with Abigail sat in the basket humming 'Raindrops keep falling on my head'. Is that not what we're led to believe: that all environmentalists ride pushbikes? Do they fuck, haven't met one yet who doesn't drive a Land Rover or a 4x4, and hack down trees for the log fire claiming they only take what's fallen from the forest: by removing the debris they are interfering with the natural environment, natural fertilizer and homes for woodland creatures. Step away from the conversation, Debbie. xx

Much-needed company, party at Chris's tomorrow for Molly's 10th birthday.

Tuesday 8th May 2014

Our 25th anniversary. xx

Still recovering from Molly's birthday yesterday. Yes, we were drinking, which fuelled the idea of a game of off-ground touch. Julie broke her toe, or more accurately Joe broke it when he jumped for the kids' see-saw and it slammed down on her foot. Me who was struggling to stand on a garden chair laughed, lost me balance, and shot over backwards and scraped all the backs of my legs. Didn't even notice the bruises till this morning. How sad am I? I've been up yonks eagerly waiting to catch Joe before he goes to work; 25 years of marriage, got to be a great gift,

Call me ungrateful, but after staying married to a man that destroys pieces of my home regularly, giving him three children thus allowing him to have four fantastic grandchildren, cook, clean and whatever else I allegedly signed up for (obviously failed to read the small print), I think I deserved a bit more recognition than a pair of silver hoops. Two tiny little circles to mark the passing of the best years of my life, given to a tight-wad. Hate that man. Obvious MLC tantrum (when it suits).

Having met me for lunch and produced 25 red roses I have

forgiven him (for today, anyway). Elizabeth and Arthur have sent us wine, so gonna have a nice quiet night in and a glass or two.

Joe had stopped to help an elderly lady (yuk) on his way to meet me for lunch. She'd crashed her scooter, no injuries but kept him there talking for ¾ of an hour about utter drivel. Ha, karma. Strangers that we meet, people who will tell you all sorts about their life presuming never to see you again, at a bus stop, during a stay in hospital in a queue, on holiday, anywhere really, never fails to shock me. I've heard some great stuff: life stories, dreams, even crimes. The best thing is when your paths do actually cross again, you can see the fear spread across their face. I've never actually been rotten enough to run over yelling, 'Hello again, remember me?' Nah, better to watch them squirm. Why do folk do this? Are they lonely? Can't keep a secret? Or is it all made up? Maybe their life is so nothing they concoct these yarns to just sound interesting for once, to have attention even if it is from a stranger this theory gets reinforced by the fact that when said stranger starts up the conversation they won't let you get a word in, it's all about them.

Old grannies are the worst (breathe, Deb): opening line is usually something like, 'I'm 99 you know. 'How aggravating is that? (1) Why would I know? (2) Don't give a shit. If they actually enjoyed still being alive I'd be impressed they've hung on this long; what they want to hear is someone say, 'Ooh, you'd never have guessed, you look so well.' This response genuinely comes from other Weebles who hope that in return for the compliment the granny will share the secret to longevity. After bigging up their age they'll move onto ailments, oh joy. Then comes the 'I've got 16 kids', all raised on a shilling, 25 grandchildren who are all at university, and 44 great grandchildren. They leave out that none of them ever visit. Wipe at eyes as they remark on fuel increases and how they'll never make it through the cold months: too tight to put the heating on, and they're all on widow's allowances, pensions, spouse's private pension.

Stop. Proper annoying myself, gone off the point I was making: telling your problems to someone you probably will never see again is similar to counselling, you get it off your chest, might even pick up some good advice confidentially. Well, that's if you don't count the other three people at bus stop who were ear-wigging, that is. I feel it's a positive thing, especially as I might be the one standing 2 foot away listening.

Wednesday 9th May 2014

What a night! Shame on us, lol!

Great evening until, having consumed a bottle and half of the very good wine (thank you to Elizabeth and Arthur) we got a bit frisky and thought we'd have a romantic soak in the tub together and finish off the wine. Forgetting that Joe, as with all members of the male species, can only bathe in water that is just above freezing I'm already sat in water as he precedes to place one foot in bath, screams (says he didn't) slips, enters the water like Shamu, nearly crushing me to death, compressing my lungs enough to wind me so I was now emanating noises like a chimpanzee on heat. The kids having heard the crash start banging on the door, and having realised that both their parents are in the bathroom together shouted we should grow up and we've apparently scarred them for life. Last memory I have of the night was Joe naked on bed with the fan blowing on his knackers. Who said romance was dead? At least this time he wasn't scowling at me. That was only because his face was frozen in a kinda stunned way.

Having spoke to Elizabeth to thank them both for the gift,

she informs me that she's stunned we even remembered our own names after drinking both bottles: the stuff is lethal and it should not only be sipped, but no more than two glasses consumed in any given evening. Thanks for the warning, lol.

Julie reckons any part of the scenario would have done her just fine. Does that girl have nothing better to do than letch over my husband?

Thursday 10th May 2014

George's 70th birthday.

Have just come back from the police station, having been there four hours waiting for them to charge me with assault. Instead I've been let off with a caution, police being on my side. It appears we share the same dislike for Exhibitionists.

Some like to walk round their homes naked; quite rightly so, it's your gaff. But put some curtains up first, then when people (members of the public going about their normal lives) walk past your window and stare cos there you are butt naked, they're not labelled weirdo's and perverts. You can't scream about breach of privacy, truth be known you want them to look or you wouldn't put it on show. The same applies when sunbathing naked in the garden: of course the old man next door is gonna peep from his upstairs window, he probably aint seen tits since he got rid of the bird table. But oh, I had to come across the worst form.

Me and Joe took the boys to the park to kick about a football, when Connor shouts 'Look!' Following his pointing finger there is a couple blatantly having sex under the willow near the duck pond. Now if doing this in public spaces where they think others can see them is how they get their rocks off, fine, but don't do it where kids go. And once busted by an irate parent, or in this case

92

a very pissed off Nan, don't make the mistake of mouthing off. At this point I smacked the geezer in the mouth so hard he went down like a lead balloon. I'm glad I still have a clean record but I would have happily done time for that arsehole. More fool them for ringing the Old Bill though: they were still at the station when we left.

Friday 11th May 2014

Jess and the kids came round for dinner as Andy has skulked off somewhere with Joe. Sam and Connor have now re-enacted me knocking out the perv 14 times now, accompanied by a badly hummed *Rocky* theme.

Sunday 13th May 2014

Alfred's 86th birthday

Joe informed me at 4pm yesterday that we were going to a fancy dress party at 7pm. Didn't appreciate it being sprung on me; he'd even bought the outfits: Superman and Batgirl. Reluctantly I got dressed and was driven to Rifles to be met by everyone in costume. Woo hoo, party was for me! Love that guy. Especially in that suit. Mmm.

Elizabeth and Arthur were the Flintstones; knowing Liz, hers was nothing short of real leopard skin. Tina and Terry came as Peter Pan and Tinkerbell. Ooh, that brought back memories: when we did that a few years back the kids said the sound of tinkling bells will haunt them forever, lol. Chloe and Paul were

Bonnie and Clyde. Oh, the list was endless. Julie came as a police officer: bet she never bought it special, probably had it in her wardrobe already. Best anniversary ever. xx

Chloe and Paul headed off early this morning to drop off her granddad's birthday presents before heading home. Elizabeth and Arthur went back to their hotel last night as they want to do some shopping up west before flying home on Monday. Vaguely remember someone telling me that Virgil was moving in with Abigail today. Oh well, can't always be good news.

It seems my grandsons no longer acknowledge me as Nan but as 'Yo! Balboa!' Scary thing is, I'm actually responding to it, lol.

Monday 14th May 2014

Bumped into Margo and the letch in town. They caught me at the pet shop. She clocked I'd bought bird seed mixed with mealworms; being the nosey tart that she is asked why on earth I'd buy such a disgusting concoction. I told her (quite loudly and proudly), 'I have great tits in the garden.' To which pervy Clive said, 'I'm sure they're great wherever you are.' Margo sniggered and said, 'What is he like?' A fucking weirdo, that's what. 'He was still flashing a leering grin as Margo stormed off, dragging him away by the arm. I reckon Tina was right years ago and he was the Parkston Park flasher.

Detoured to Mum's on way back. Hmm, teach me for not calling first: sat there on the sofa with a leg elevated, pointing at three red lumps on her shin, was Chris. Flea bites! As ever has misheard the guy and has told Mum its phlebitis. Didn't even take my coat off, just said goodbye and left. One day that girl's gonna actually get something real and the shock will kill her. Or me.

We teamed up with Tina, Terry, Julie and Charles for a spooky night at an old abandoned alms house. We were greeted by the two mediums running the show, and soon us and the other 'hunters' were hustled into the hall where they proceed to guide us through the history and the demise of its residents. The centre of its gloom was of the orphan girl Annie who was walled up in the kitchen for stealing an apple. Her slow, fading voice is said to haunt the hallways forever more. Apart from the odd creak and a cold draft the whole evening was becoming a bit lame, so a break was suggested. Tea and sandwiches consumed, and tales from others of their ghostly encounters told, we resumed and headed off towards the kitchen. Heard Joe snicker as the medium asked for the fourth time, 'Annie, are you there?' Each time sounding more desperate, probably scared the only thing they'd hear tonight was people demanding a refund.

Was about to move on when someone said, 'What's that sound?' Everybody took the same intake of breath and in the silence was the faint sound of a little girl's voice. Panic ensued, lol. Be careful what you wish for. It got louder and we could easily hear the words to 'Twinkle Twinkle Little Star'. I said aloud what others wanted to, that this was the most creepy demonic thing they'd heard. Then it was gone. We felt it was definitely a much-needed fag break next. Returned to the hall, got our jackets and was about to light a fag when she was back and clearly in the room with us, the singing louder than ever. Two of the women in the group started crying, Joe and Terry were now practically sharing the same chair. All eyes were on me.

If I'm honest I was on the verge of bolting when I realised I knew that voice. Daisy? Reaching into my pocket and retrieving my mobile, there was a message from Andy: 'Hey, did you love it? We recorded it earlier and I changed your message alert to play it. 'As I've said before, nowt funnier than fear on a person's face, lol. Try eighteen at once.

Wednesday 16th May 2014

Mutley vets 10am.

Positioned on very thick plastic sheeting and won't be given any bribe treats beforehand.

Friday the 18th May 2014

Is it me, or does everyone living here expect others to clear up after them? Oh, I get it, 'others' is me, then.

Another thing, why oh why do we get badgered by our kids to give them a house key? They insist they're responsible enough to have one and that we're insulting them by even thinking that they're not, yet no sooner do we relent, the bastards never have it on them, or they lose it which they somehow try and blame on us, cos obviously I've got nothing better to do than hide keys, unless I indeed have put them in the 'safe place', then fair do's. A revolving front door would be easier than me getting up and down to open it.

Saturday 19th May 2014

Leg wax 2pm.

Legs nicely waxed. What's the point of women waxing the top lip? Can't say I've noticed very often when a woman's got a moustache, but I can always spot a waxed one, strange!

BBQ tomorrow for Joe's birthday, Chloe and Paul have arrived at her mum's, and Elizabeth and Arthur are enroute to the hotel in Knightsbridge.

Monday 21st May 2014

Joe's 39th birthday.

The BBQ was a success: no mishaps or trips to the emergency room, gotta be a first. Abigail blew us out to take Virgil for lunch at Sandra's and her dad's.

Chloe and Paul left at five this morning, Elizabeth and Arthur left late last night as they're meeting Edward for lunch today before they head off back to the Big Apple. Just realized it's Monday and Chris has gone swimming with Abigail and Penny rather than the docs: she must be ill, lol. Julie will be around about six-ish to give Joe his gifts: heaven help us. Then I and he are heading off to dinner for his birthday.

Wednesday 23rd May 2014

Hairdresser 5pm.

Funniest thing ever! Virgil wants me to join his jogging club.

Funny for two reasons: (1)Does he actually think I'd wanna be in his company?(2)Me jogging? Seriously? Exercise to me is like garlic to a vampire.

Thursday 24th May 2014

Was looking at Leigh earlier and was remembering what we got up to at their age. Mate! That's scary.

Ooh ha ah hee! We was having a nice quite night in watching a film when there was a sound like something had fallen into the waste paper bin, which was next to Joe. In a panic, thinking he'd dropped one of his fruit pastilles he leans over to look: screams, literally. Then runs out to the kitchen. A little startled myself I sneak up to have a look, and sitting at the bottom is a mouse, shaking. I proceeded toward the back garden with mousey; bearing in mind it's only about twenty steps to the patio doors it was taking forever, as every four steps I had to stop cos I couldn't breathe for laughing. I was not sure who was more traumatised: Joe at the sight of the mouse, or the mouse receiving an ear-splitting scream from an enormous, very butch man.

Oh ha, I told you we had a mouse.

Friday 25th May 2014

Girls' night Tina's 7pm.

Much-needed night round Tina's after the day I had. I'm not superstitious, but… ! Spent 45 minutes driving around the streets looking for a magpie. Chris had seen only the one in the garden and was convinced she'd have bad luck. I humoured her and went searching for another, as her bad luck ends up somehow my problem anyway.

The girls had me repeat the story of the mouse at least three times, lol. It's never gonna get old.

Saturday 26th May 2014

Another disappointing thing that comes with age: you stop getting good crusty scabs. Kids always get the best ones. Those that don't pick scabs would be thinking 'filth', and yeah, maybe so, but carefully plucking away at said crusty patch would keep us quiet for hours – or at least until it bled.

BBQ again tomorrow, low key, just us.

Monday 28th May 2014

BBQ was most enjoyed yesterday. Only ripple in my pond was when Terry texted Joe to say Virgil was an amazing surfer and a cool guy. Both couples have gone to Cornwall and thought they'd hook up for the day at the beach. Hang on, I'm sitting in 'care' chair right now. That man could not be cool if he fell into liquid hydrogen. Chris skulked off to Mum's around nine last night, complaining she's had a pain in her neck for days (welcome to my world).Dad had to call the emergency doctor, as Chris had a massive lump that was now oozing green shit. By all accounts it looked like an abscess but turns out it was a bee sting that had gone unnoticed for days and gone manky. Only her.

The fair was in town today so we took the little ones. Sam won a goldfish. I could have bought one for £2, total attempts to win it cost £11, how convenient that the stall holder had bowls for sale +£6 this triggered cries of ' I want one!' Two bowls and four fish later, not much change from £50.

Joe not getting that I had to get a fish for each grandchild as Rosie is only six months old. What sort of woman would I be if not equal towards them all? Andy understood: well, said it's my school of thought and I'm a nutter.

Jessica's adamant that she'll be having no filthy bowl in her house, so they're here.

Tuesday 29th May 2014

Went for a Burton down the stairs last night. Only four steps from the bottom, slipped grabbed the hand rail and stooped backwards like an extra from the *Matrix*. My feet were running on the spot as I tried desperately not to land on my arse, mid-flailing I caught my foot in Tony's sports bag, the one I'd put there earlier under the sad illusion that he would actually take it up, so foot in nylon bag on carpeted stairs I skidded to ground level, each footfall sounding like the guy in the military band with the big drum banging. Forgot to let go of the rail so as gravity wrenched my carcass downwards I had the pleasure of feeling all the muscle and tendons tear in my shoulder. Before I hit the floor I could hear Tony and Leigh upstairs wetting themselves, as was I. Joe, who is not so spritely at the best of times, was in the garden, heard the banging and came galloping at full speed like a startled gazelle, looking terrified as to what state I would be in. Started trying to drag me up, whispering, 'Come on now, before the kids see. 'Between the pain, snot and tears I nearly laughed myself sick. Why don't men laugh? Well, if Joe's answer is anything to go on, be afraid: 'A woman is the key holding the family together, so if she cacks it, how's he gonna cope?'Gee and there was stupid me thinking it was cos he cared xx

Wednesday 30th May 2014

Connor's fish died. He wasn't very impressed with the 'Yippee, one down three to go. 'Guilt has led me to the pet shop, lucky me! It was buy one, get one free. Perched on the counter in the kitchen the 3foot tank now sits with the annoying silent (*only if you're deaf*) pump with seven ropey goldfish. A short service will be held this afternoon for Godzilla.

Thursday 31st May 2014

Chloe and Liz arrive London.

Julie popped round after work and stated 'Not only have you've been lumbered with the fish, you have now progressed to a tank, you'll be digging a pond soon. 'Hell will freeze over first: I paid three grand to have the garden landscaped. I immediately defended myself and threw down the gauntlet of 'Fifty quid says I won't, so put your money where your mouth is, woman.' Shit, she took the bet, then texted Elizabeth and Chloe. Elizabeth, not one to partake in gambling, said she knew a sure thing so she too has taken the bet. Chloe too. I take offence at the lack of belief from my mates.

Girls' night at mine tomorrow. Might tell them all to fuck off xx

Saturday 2nd June 2014

Chloe and Elizabeth both made it to girls' night last night. Wished I didn't have it here as I had the piss taken out of me all-night about the tank. Chloe headed back this morning. Elizabeth is staying until tomorrow so we're going to squander some cash up Oxford Street, get some dinner. The boys are holding poker at ours so I won't be rushing back.

Tuesday 5th June 2014

Sunday was uneventful. Yesterday began with the arrival of 'pond man' at 8.30am.

Note to self: Really must join that assertiveness class. And for the so-called mates, the cheques are in the post.

I waited with bated breath that pond man would be a fit young stud. Seriously, who was I kidding? Fit for fuckall. Young? Sixty-two if he's a day. He kept winking at me, and I'm pretty certain he was wearing a wig. (I take that back.) Guess this is what happens when you let the husband pick workman: a man is not gonna invite a young, attractive sex god into your home and leave him unattended in your care. After all, let's just say I am having a mid-life crisis, but hey! That don't mean I'd sleep with some bloke because he's young and trim. Took photo and sent it to Julie. Julie commented I could be in there if I played my cards right, which caused me to ask if 'monogamy' means anything to her. Answer: 'Aint that a board game where you buy streets?'

Baby's party had far too many kids at it, lol. And I defiantly had far too much wine. Give a shit? Nope.

How aggravating that when the other half can't open a jar (real hit to masculinity) and you do it, he always has to pipe up, 'I loosened it.'

Elizabeth and Arthur's anniversary.

Elizabeth emailed me to say that guilt had got the better of her and she confessed her affair to Arthur. Shockingly (only to Elizabeth, not the rest of us), he has owned up to knocking off the Embryo. Shocker number two was instead of separating they are gonna continue with all the relationships. WTF? Gonna need a bit of time to get my brain round that one.

Why, when you stub your big toe, does your brain give you enough time to think 'Oh shit!' before the pain sets in? Pain enough to bring you to your knees and start gagging. Or maybe it's the brain that screams just before shutting down, thus leaving you to deal with the pain on your own. Also, why do we hold it like our very life depends on it, pausing only long enough to sneak a peek at the very hot throbbing digit concealed within your fist. I definetely came off worse than the coffee table last night at Chris's.

Awoke this morning to cluttering and banging. Stumbled - well, hobbled, as toe is still throbbing- downstairs and quickly realised why I have Joe so heavily insured: he wanted to attach the pond pump to the wall so was knee deep in the pond armed with an electric drill. Yes, I said electric drill, in hand. I'm not writing this from Bermuda so yes, he made it. In Joe's defence, he needs insuring against me most of the time. Err, I must have hit more than my toe if I'm sympathising with him.

Sunday 10th June 2014

Chris rang late last night screaming there was a pervert in her back garden making weird noises near the window. Joe drove round there and found nothing. He did a thorough search of the garden but found no trace of any intruders. He went back today and fitted locks on her windows.

Abigail is taking Virgil to lunch with the parents again, lol. If I know Sandra, it won't be long before she'll put him in his place, lol

Bollocks. Chloe texted to say her mum thinks he's wonderful. What's wrong with everybody?

Monday 11th June 2014

Chris was at the docs this morning with palpitations. Gonna forgive her that one: if I thought I had a weirdo in my garden I'd be having them as well.

Joe asked me to phone the AA this morning to check his expiry date on his policy, and I got the really posh bird who kept asking me to repeat what I'd said. How insulting! I was born and bred in London so it's inevitable that I speak this way: in a nutshell, 'common as cat shit'. I have been picked on all my life for the way I speak, mainly by idiots who speak like they've got their thumb up their arse.

The argument is always the same: who's right and who aint? I watched a programme once that had investigated the whole issue thoroughly and the experts stated that the way I speak is in fact 'proper' English. All of society who speaks with a plum in their mouth is actually working very hard to vocalise in this manner because it requires an unnatural formation of the sounds. I watch people and it seems too much like hard work to talk posh. For me to have a good chin wag I open my gob and the words easily flow out, I can easily slip from one subject to another, whereas the posh type are concentrating so hard to pronounce every 'T 'they don't seem to be enjoying the conversation. What's the point of that, then? Wot ya see iz wot u get. This, it seems, applies to all classes.

Tuesday 12th June 2014

Yesterday saw me being judged for the way I talk, then today I got eye-balled by the 'larger lady 'in the clothes shop when I asked the assistant if she had the jeans I was holding in an 8.Should I go there? Yes. I have never been on a diet, have never needed to diet, I am one of those hated women who eat anything that's not nailed down and never gain an ounce. Larger people are not the only ones who are judged for their size, sneered at, taunted. I've been accused of being bulimic, anorexic, slagged off, ridiculed, been made to feel guilty, spiteful, arrogant and even ashamed. I am one of only a few in my entire family this size; the average is big. I will offer words of support to anyone who says they're dieting, note the changes, comment how well they're doing... in return I've been attacked with snide looks and spiteful comments, like, 'How would you know what it's like?' Fair do's, I don't know what it's like to watch what I eat, but I do know what it's like to be judged by appearance and to be verbally attacked for my dress size.

While I think of it, I can remember my Nan telling me about a medical scandal many eons ago about the miracle diet tablet which turned out to have a tapeworm egg in it. Gross, I know. I remarked to my mum, 'What would you do if you had said parasite prescribed by your doc?' To which she replied, 'I'd wait until I'd lost 2 stone, then have it removed.' Still makes me smile.

Anyway, I believe there is too much focus on weight, and size(yeah, easy for me to say).But it's true, everywhere we look, magazines, movies, TV we're surrounded by beauty and perfection, rippling gym-toned bodies, designer clothing. Amazingly, even though every supermodel who's been interviewed will say how all their advertising has been airbrushed; most of us have seen the photographic evidence of these people, warts and all, and we know that like the rest of us they look as rough as shark shit too. So why do we still believe that we can torture ourselves and we'll look just like their pictures? Money: the industry know how to play on low self-esteem, no matter how ridiculous we may look, how much it will cost or how crap we will feel never achieving the look, as long as we're lining their pockets.

This is another area us petites share with larger women: clothing. Correct me if I'm wrong, but when you do find a store that sells their larger sizes, and in my case petite, has anyone noticed the serious lack of variety and fashion? Larger clothing borders on retro hippie wear, or something your great aunt would wear to a funeral; small peeps are OK if you work in an office: trousers, smart blouse, cardigan. Apparently it appears from the apparel that us types don't want to look cool or sexy. Obviously never socialize, or have someone to look good for. apparently the average UK dress size for women is a 16, so why then if I browse the shops do they have14/16s always in the sales? They should have flown out the door. The only thing I ever enjoy about clothes shopping is the garments that state 'one size fits all'. I don't think so, luv: said garment is either going to hang off you like a potato sack or fit so tight it makes your arse look like a bank robber.

Back to the issue of the weight itself, there are large people who through no fault of their own have only have to look at food to gain pounds, and hand on heart I do genuinely feel for them :if I want something I have it, based on that alone I know it must be hard. There are health issues for all of us, for some losing weight is paramount to their well-being. skinny women have to maintain their weight or would be very ill. That may sound patronising, but if I was to skip a meal I lose weight immediately; when I get about of flu or sickness and my appetite is gone, I still have to force myself to eat.

So to be deemed having an eating disorder, hurts. Especially when you seek support for ways to gain weight; nothing to do with vanity, just simply because being small made me feel tired, weak, washed out, and caught every bug and germ that got passed about. The responses: 'Are you taking the piss?', 'Perhaps you need professional help', 'Admitting there's a problem is a good start'...the list is endless. Did I respond like that when they went on a diet? No, I was supportive, encouraging, considerate. Some say it's the stress of the dieting that makes them treat you like that. Nah, it isn't. If the same comments had been made by a larger-built friend or relative, they would have been appreciated. I've now resigned myself to not get pulled into these conversations anymore: if someone says they're on a diet I just avoid them. Much easier, because in these situations us smaller peeps can't even defend ourselves from the spite.

Overweight people are accused of self-infliction: in other words, they're just greedy, And for fear of getting lynched, I think some are, the same as there are skinny people who starve themselves on purpose. There is a regular at the bakers who is huge and will tell anyone she has serious health issues because of her weight, yet she will regularly order a Cornish pasty, two sausage rolls, a bacon bap and a fresh cream scone, always followed up with, 'Oh and a Diet Coke. 'No need: this is the women whose leggings are stretched so tight over her bottom half you could read the label on the inside; which, much to my amusement, says 'One size fits all'. Any bigger and she'll end up one of them who can't even get out of bed.

WTF? They didn't get that size overnight; the signs were clearly there long before. How do they afford the large amounts of food? They obviously don't work. And most importantly, who's feeding them? Isn't that abuse? Cos without someone bringing the food to where the person lay, they would go without. One story I read, the husband in this case said it was out of love; she would cry and beg, saying she was hungry. Was he then not killing her with kindness?.A lot of big people will say, 'I like being like this, I feel comfortable with myself.' Cool, then why look at me when we pass in a swimming pool, like I'm the scourge of society? Whenever I see someone who is large I pass no judgement, I don't automatically presume they've got no self-control over their consumption. So don't look at me and think I have an eating disorder; we have more in common than we think.

Wednesday 13th June 2014

Had Chris on the phone again last night insisting the peeping tom was back. Another pointless search by Joe who now is convinced Chris is definitely off her nut.

Went round Andy's this afternoon. Sam's hamster not looking none too clever. I've phoned the vets and I will take him tomorrow morning.

Hang on! Why me?

Thursday 14th June 2014

Penny and Mark's anniversary.

Vet 8.45am hamster.

Organised a funeral today. Joe dug the hole, I was pall bearer and vicar. Sam's beloved hamster Bucky has passed away after six years, quite a feat: they usually snuff it within three. In the rain we stood, the grandchildren reciting the Lord's Prayer, me and Joe trying not to snicker. Turns out poor Bucky had a tumour so we'd had to have him put to sleep. Sam had said he didn't want me to bring the body home, so the vet disposed of him. By mid-afternoon the child has a breakdown, declaring we must give Bucky a proper funeral, so we did what all decent grandparents do and lied, said we got the body and here he was already wrapped and sealed in a make shift but, most importantly, child-proof coffin (shoebox covered in large amounts of Sellotape). This was the best-attended funeral for a hamster-sized stone, may it rest in peace. xx

Julie was quite miffed that were so quick to judge her and proceeded to point out that she would at least be upfront with what she'd done. Lying to babies: shocking! And it's gonna cost me to keep her from telling the kids when they're older. My only defence, that I do what I do outta love. Will admit it was quite low, and I do feel slight pang of guilt. Will pay hush money, Julie can name her price as long as it has nothing to do with my husband. Elizabeth, although she despises lying (ha ha, yeah, OK), agreed that on this occasion lying was the right thing to do.

Friday 15th June 2014

Joe has fitted a camera outside Chris's back garden after she called again and this time held the phone to her window, and I could hear the spine-chilling grunting and groaning. Poor Chris, even her own sister thought it was all in her head; I feel really bad. The police have been informed and have said as soon as she hears anything to call, and they will send assistance immediately. How creepy.

Sunday 17th June 2014

Father's Day.

Had a shit day yesterday, literally. Someone had walked dog crap through the house. When I say 'someone 'I can safely narrow that down to someone with testicles, as women look where they're walking.

For Father's Day, and to make up for dragging Joe out of bed several times because of her peeping tom, Chris invited us to dinner. All was going well until she pricked the chicken and it exploded, I swear this family is cursed, Hmm, not whole family, just Christine.

Chris's pervert was caught tonight. Having called us, then the police, we all arrived at the same time. There were three armed officers who crept round the back, and on their order the garden was flooded with light from the helicopter hovering overhead. Spotlighted and with three assault rifles pointed at them sat two hedgehogs, humping.

Connor's class assembly 9am.

Happily attended Connor's class assembly this morning. The head teacher made an announcement: 'Would the parents of a certain pupil refrain them from telling the other children that two ladybirds stuck together are not sexing each other up. 'Like many other mums and Nan's in attendance, me and Jessica stifled a snicker until Connor stands up (still on stage) and shouts 'That's me!', whilst frantically waving at us. Most definitely feel Julie had something to do with this. Not that I think Connor needs any encouragement, as he does just fine under his own steam, love him.

Hairdresser 5pm.

Ooh, Suzanne rang me last night. She'd spent Monday night

at the Irish Bar on Broad Street, reckons she'd met the man of her dreams until he opened his mouth and his breath nearly knocked her over. Lol, why is it when someone mentions breath you have to fight the urge to breath into your palm and check your own. That's what's frightening about halitosis: you'll be the last to know. Let's face it, there's no nice or compassionate way to tell someone. Hmm, unless they're your least favourite person, then I'm sure you'd relish the idea of telling them.

Thankfully the people closest to me don't have the breath of a thousand camels; as awful as it would be to wrap them and myself in embarrassment, I would tell them, on the quiet, or at worst leave them an anonymous note. Surely no one would let them go about their lives always wondering why others avoid conversations and normal social interaction with them.

Failing that, if you can't face speaking up to someone you care deeply about yourself, borrow a small child from a relative or friend and force 'the stinky one' to interact with said child. I guarantee the child will sort it, Approx four or five years old, they don't beat around the bush, they'll say it straight: 'Your breath smells. 'This should be enough for the person in question to get it checked out.

Suzanne said it weren't the odour left by food or even smoking. Nah, them smells usually vanish with a good brush of the teeth. We're talking about the tear-jerking, throat-tightening waft that could strip paint, lol.

Peter from the office two floors up from Julie's office got reprimanded when his colleagues reported him to personnel that after travelling up several floors in a lift with him and his breath, which they said had taken over the entire air capacity, they were not only distressed but they actually felt they had been assaulted.

Poor bloke, but how funny!

Chloe arrived at her mum's yesterday and got to mine around four. Girls' night was pretty low key as we had no Tina as she and Mark are still on safari in Africa, and Penny and Mark have taken the kids to Devon. Julie said she'd spoken to Elizabeth and that she and Arthur were at a tennis tournament at the Batemans estate. Guessing Liz hasn't told Julie about Rico; as for the Embryo, I hope she shows some discretion. Julie has jetted off to Jersey with Charles this morning. Err, hello, why am I the only person not on holiday?

Chloe's staying till Sunday. We did consider popping round Chris's today until Jo said she had Abigail and Virgil for the day, so we've taken up Andy and Jess's offer of lunch at theirs.

Connor pushed Jessica to the limits at lunch today; he couldn't get his own way and declared he was leaving home. I reassured Jessica they all have these paddy's at this age, and best not to bite his bait, so together we calmly watched, as it was kinda cute to watch a five-year-old indignantly pack his bag. Playing along, I said he couldn't take his toys with him cos I'd bought them. His head spun like *The Exorcist* and he screamed, 'Santa bought them, not you!' Joe intervened in the nick of time as I was about to yell back, 'I was Santa, the Easter Bunny and the fucking Tooth Fairy, ya little ingrate!'

Note to self: Only write 'From Santa' on one of the Christmas pressies.

Chloe laughed her arse off, she reckons Connor's just like me. Don't know what she means (fluttering of eyelids, sickly smile). xx

Thought I had an emergency on me hands this morning: I turned over in bed and thought I saw a hair sticking out of Joe's back. Freaked me right out. Dirty ears being the most repulsive thing in the universe is followed by back hair. Julie always goes one step further, liking her men smooth and hairless all over. Mate, as if the giblets aint ugly enough, she wants them looking like a shell-less tortoise. Hairless may be her preference, but let's not kid ourselves here: Julie takes on all comers.

After dropping Chloe at the station, me and Joe picked up Chris and went to the Sunday market where Joe spotted and bought Sam a pogo stick.

Betty 86th birthday.

Penny and Julie had lunch at their mum's for the Nan's birthday, Julie got to mine about four, and so began a very shit day. We have just got back from Accident and Emergency with me sporting a temporary cast on my right arm, as I have broken my bloody wrist.

So embarrassing. I was gonna tell the doctors how I'd been injured saving the cat from a 70 foot tree when Joe whipped past me and informed them loudly how I couldn't refuse the challenge when he'd said I couldn't bounce at least five jumps on Sam's pogo stick (he being extremely talented on said stick). So's not to be outdone, by *him*, up I climbed and managed four really pathetic jumps and landed on the concrete. The pain was horrendous, within half an hour me arm was double the size, so having endured four hours of everyone from nurses to radiologists taking the piss I'm now home feeling sorry for myself. Worse than the pain is the fact that Joe was right, and is better than me on the poxy thing. Lectured by Julie (with a smirk) that I should learn to rise above such challenges. Then, both of them having a good laugh at my expense, she then demonstrated that even she can do a good five minutes on a pogo, in heels. Yeah, wonder where she learnt that trick. xx

Just got a text from Chloe: 'Just heard the news, lmfao.' Yeah, cheers, pal.

Roll on four weeks.

Tuesday 26th June 2014

Hospital 9.30am.

Back to hospital this morning, endured yet more laughter from medical staff, it seems I have broken wrist in such a stupid place the X-ray isn't clear enough for them to set it in plaster: if they do, it will lead to re-breaking it at a later date. I don't think so.

Tomorrow they're sending me to be injected with radioactive substance that will then show a clearer picture on a special scanner. Because I'll be nuclear I'm not allowed near small children, so hubby not allowed near me, lol.

Due to this morning's stress I have again found myself in possession of 26 new pairs of knickers - on sale mind ya. They will be put in the drawer with the other 200 pairs I haven't worn yet. We need many for many occasions: comfy, hit by a bus, and seductive. That's the best excuse I've got for this fetish.

Nuclear injection 10am.

Lunch with Chris 12pm.

Procedure worked. I am now sporting a bright yellow cast, with the warning it will itch like mad and under no circumstances am I to shove things up it to scratch. Ooo err Mrs.

Chris cancelled lunch date with me: she don't like the sound of radiation, doesn't believe me that the cast was yellow before it was attached to me. She's gonna ring the NHS helpline: she wants to know if she should be concerned for although she loves me dearly it's not enough to have her hair fall out being in my company. Then the stupid cow said, 'I know, why don't you just paint a red cross on the front door?'Can't believe I had to explain to the div that a red cross was for the plague, not radioactivity. Chris paused, gasped inwards, and screamed 'You have the plague? OMG I told you that pet rat of Leigh's didn't look right!'Insistent that I should have it put to sleep. Of course it didn't look right, it's a bleeding gerbil. Der!

Andy's 25th birthday.

Dentist 9am.

Browsing a magazine at the dentists today I read an article that said 99% of adults confessed to having masturbated at some time. Who did they ask? Did this include women? I've never met a female whose owned up to it: sex aids, yes; but hands, no. Even blokes I could count on one hand it's not something you'd admit to your best mate, so surely you're not gonna tell some dude taking a survey. No, I daren't ask Julie, too much information and all that, *no*!

If these stats are accurate then let's hope they don't all decide to have a go at the same time or the earth really is gonna move. It went on to say that marriages have broken down because of it, where the wife has taken it personal: she has felt that she must be failing in the sexual satisfaction department; or because the bloke does it so much he now can't get it up for her. Someone I knew welcomed this scenario with the opinion it saved her the job.

Myths surrounding masturbation include going blind will give you acne, make you sterile, and my favourite: you'll get hairy palms. My guess is these were all started by mothers.

Me and Joe babysitting as Andy and Jess are going out to celebrate.

School reunion tomorrow night

Friday 29th June 2014

School reunion 7pm.

Just got back from Chris's. Got the phone call at 5.30 this morning, she was hysterical. I rushed over there in a panic, lucky I never rang an ambulance on route, there was no blood or broken bones, but... nits!

Two nits and one flea, to be exact.

Her only saving grace for scaring me half to death was that her reaction was quite normal. Good God, we have something in common.

Let's be honest, someone only has to mention their kids may have nits and it'll send a ripple of disgust and horror through us mums. The first time Andy got them I rang Nan in tears, telling her I was a skank. When she'd finished laughing she came round armed with conditioner and a comb and de-flead him. We all get told that having nits don't mean you're a dirty person, but that goes out the window when ya see them on *your* child's head, evil-looking little bastards (fleas, not kids; hmm, actually, both). Itching just thinking about them. My heart goes out to 'Nitty Nora': every school's got one. These poor kids are running alive with them and the parents don't seem to do anything about it. That amount wouldn't be just itchy it would be dementing. Leigh had a Nora in her class: she was so riddled you could see them running over the hair. Theresa, being discreet but still wanting to highlight the fact, said, 'I think you've got something in your hair. 'To which the little girl replied, 'It's just nits. 'The mother said she refuses to deal with it, as what's the point, she'll only get them again. Now that's a skank.

While that girl was still in school all our girls had their hair soaked with conditioner and pulled into pony tails, which works. Because of kids like these the rest of us were the ones constantly de-fleaing our kids. Several of us mums confronted the head teacher, only to be told they couldn't suspend the child pending removal of parasites; neither could they insist the parent treats the child as this is discrimination. What bollocks, especially when Theresa said she would keep her daughter home until this was sorted and got told she could be prosecuted for intentional truancy. World's gone mad. Forget about how we feel for a minute, what about Nitty Nora? Nits has got the same effect as leprosy: left untreated the child will be alienated by everyone in the playground, scratched from all party invites, and will miss out on vital social interaction; and let's be honest, there's no one as cold or less forgiving as primary school kids. From experience most of the spitefulness that comes from kids, mouths came via their own parents, who are frightened of being whispered about. Believe me, little kids need no help throwing petrol on fires. Yeah, Elizabeth. xx

Four coffees later, Baby was flea free, Christine calm, and I'm itching. Cheers!

Chloe should be here around five; more than enough time to get her to check my hair. Shouldn't be hard, seeing as it's not a full head.

Saturday 30th June 2014

Leg wax 2pm.

Poker night.

After spending an hour being checked by Chloe for cooty's we made it to the school reunion last night. Couldn't be asked to go, but glad I did, we had a blinding time. Julie, the inevitable robotics. Mate? Please. Classmates and old flames, all of us ageing quite gracefully with exception to the 'It 'guy, Steve who was once Mr Perfect in his day. I say 'once' as he's now bald as a badger with a pot belly. Sadly, I don't think he knows this and he still tried to pull me. I got many compliments on my slim waistline, little do they know all credit goes to Joe for the untold stress he causes me, lol. Julie left early with some guy called Gerry. None of us remembers his face from school; really attractive, so we reckon he must have been one of those nerds that evolved later in life. I've texted Julie for details but haven't had any reply yet.

I felt a bit gutted when my ex breezed in looking nearly as good as he did 20 years ago. Cheered up slightly when someone pointed out his wife: big fat bird. Cheered up even more when I realised it was Donna, the original Barbie and top girl from school. Gloating subsided for pity when he bought drinks over to our table with his mobile number under my glass. How ironic, she was the reason he dumped me.

We had such a great night that about 30 of us have organised to meet up again. I suspect my mid-life crisis is taking over: who knows, maybe I'll wear the stripper boots. xx

Off shopping for Andy's birthday BBQ.

Positives: No hangover.
Negatives: Cos drinking arm is in a cast.

Monday 2nd July 2014

Shopping.

BBQ yesterday went well. Tina and Terry fresh back from Africa gave Andy a fertility statue. Joe not impressed, as he said he can't handle anymore grandkids at the moment. Elizabeth got back from her trip to Hawaii with Rico; how's that discreet?

I rang Julie three times yesterday, leaving messages. Still had no reply, hmm what's going on? Chris said she'd seen her leaving the supermarket last night but she drove off before Chris could talk to her, so I know she's alive.

Chloe left around ten this morning to get back to the farm.

Just back from craft store with pack of knitting needles, arm itching like fuck. I know I shouldn't but God it feels good. The itching was almost as bad as thrush. Oh ha ha, shut up, nothing is ever as bad as thrush.

Not sure if we should be worried. It's Julie's turn for girlie night on Friday, so will get to the bottom of it then.

Tuesday 3rd July 2014

Oh my *God*! Julie is fine, not sure if we are. After leaving the reunion things apparently got really steamy in the car park, but Gerry had said he wanted to do things proper so they went back to his place. They drank champagne, lit candles, and he undressed her slowly, paying close attention to every detail of her body. Julie then started to do the same; said she was so charged she practically tore his kit off – to discover he had no giblets. He was a she, not some birth defect, but a woman. Hence why we didn't recognise him... her... she was *Geraldine* from Mr Baker's biology class. We'd were stunned into silence, except for Julie who declared it was the most erotic night of her life and that she *will* be doing it again. Poor Chris came for lunch. I filled her in and she threw up. Each to their own I guess; does this make Julie a lesbian? Apart from the deception on Gerry's behalf, I gotta say Gerry is a stunning-looking man.

Wednesday 4th July 2014

Joe went fishing and forgot the sun lotion and is now glowing from face to waistline. I have duly lectured him on the stupidity of this and have since lovingly rubbed copious amounts of moisturiser into his skin. I done it of course cos I love him, but more importantly because I know it will aid the dead skin to shed in better strips.

Note to self: Remember to pin hubby to floor in approx three days when skin will be ready for peeling.

Joe's dad Pat's 70th birthday.

Melissa from five doors down is pregnant. Ah, bless, she's only 17 but very mature. News reached Beryl the Beak, who of course was quick to condemn her and entire generations of her family for being sluts. Apart from telling her to mind her own business I said to her I know many women who had planned babies at the 'right time', when 'financially secure', and within marriage, and some of them are seriously crap mothers. Age, I don't think is an issue. Beryl has a very short memory, if you take the age of her eldest daughter away from her real age (tells everyone she's 68 when really she's 62) this makes her 14 when she became pregnant. *Slut*! Lol. You know, for a woman to add years on her age, she has to be hiding summit. Mum was at school with her, she was known back then as Back Draft Beryl, on account of her never wearing knickers. And hanging around the fire station after dark. In the summer of 1952 she was sent on a visit to her Aunty Jean in Suffolk, returned three years later with husband Chuck and two kids under the age of four. Hmm, not rocket science. Chuck was a nice old guy though, whenever she'd confiscate our balls that went into her garden he would sneak them out and give them back on his way to work. This is how these nasty old bags end up with nice guys... shotgun, lol. Chuck was 29 when he dabbled on his shift at the fire station and had to marry her. Sure he only died to get some peace.

We're off to Joe's parents tonight for dinner with the family to celebrate Dad's birthday, probably end up at Flannigan's.

Before I went to Julie's last night I was having a visual rant about that sister of mine whilst dishing up dinner: she and the girls are off to Florida for two weeks and she's packed and unpacked 16 times and rang me five times to do a checklist.

Visual rant = arms flailing in emphasis of emotion – in this case annoyance – involves pointing and the like. Unbeknown to me a piece of hot meat pie was on the end of the knife. Joe appeared in the doorway pretending to give a toss at what I was saying, suddenly covers his right eye, screams (says he didn't). I didn't stay in and endure another evening spent with him glaring at me with the good eye, the other one was covered with some manky slice of Arctic Roll I found at bottom of the freezer amongst all the loose peas.

Note to self: Must buy Joe an icepack or two. Or he could take up Julie's offer of pain diversion. Slut. xx

I eventually got to Julie's for girlie night and had to endure Chris keep asking, 'What have I forgot?'

This is why I drink.

Joe arrived at Julie's at midnight to pick Chris and the girls up as he was on airport duty. Stupidly asked me if I want to come for the ride. If looks could kill I'd be a rich woman right now.

I breathe a little easier today. Ah, peace.

Knocked Joe out, lol. xx The fan belt on the Hoover broke yet again and as he bent to look I thought it'd be helpful and flip it over. Clunk. Then thud, the sound of the handle smacking him at great force between the eyes, knocking him to the ground rendering him unconscious. Coma only lasted a few seconds, unlike my laughter that rang through the house for hours. I fear I've been living with Mr Calamity for so long he's rubbing off on me. I thank you.

If the tight bastard bought me a new one this could have been avoided.

Joe football.

Shopping.

Yippee, *pick* day. xx

Woo hoo, pick day. xx

Now I know I'm not alone in this and it does seem to be a predominantly female thing… Joe thinks I'm scum, but will sit there anyway, letting me have my way as I delight in peeling his back. It's the noise as you tear the skin away from the body, kinda crackly whoosh. Actually makes the mouth water. Ultimate goal is to get whole big strips and he knows better than to fidget. If Chris was here she'd say I have issues(fuck me, that'd be rich coming from her). I say don't knock it till you try it.

Roll on five o'clock.

Suntrap with Sam 9am.

We were at a BBQ party at Michael and John's last night.

Neighbour Mary and toothless wonder John was there. Me having drunk loads was happily telling Mary she should dump his sorry arse, when he turned to me and said, 'If I was your husband I'd poison your food.' I politely replied, 'If I were your wife I'd happily eat it.'

Sam had Sun Trap today; they were given a list of things to find, i.e. something sticky, prickly, rough etc (should have taken Julie with me). The teacher has had a reality check, realising she needs to review the list or to be more specific, as two kids under the order of 'something white' returned with dried-out dog turds stuck to their worksheet, and as for the 'something living', Sam had Sello-taped a live earwig to his sheet.

Thursday 12th July 2014

Juliette popped round with her eldest, Claire. I couldn't wait for them to leave, so resumed picking Joe's skin. Poor Joe ended up laying on the floor with myself, Leigh, Juliette and Claire hanging off his back like apes fighting over a banana. Ahh, love him. xx

Saturday 14th July 2014

Yesterday was Friday the 13th and the gods shone on me as Chris is still in Florida. Yesterday was also the last day of school before the summer holidays begin; somehow summers always seemed longer and sunnier when we were kids.

Elizabeth and Arthur set off on a cruise on the company yacht. Alright for some.

Girls' night at Tina's. With the absence of Chris and Abigail an intelligent conversation was had about marriage. Just as it began to remind us all of the happy reasons we did it for, Julie killed the topic with one sentence: 'Wedding rings are the world's smallest handcuffs.'

Sunday 15th July 2014

Margaret and Pat's anniversary.

No cooking today, off to the Piper for lunch, courtesy of Joe and his bros for their mum and dad's wedding anniversary.

The internet is playing up constantly. I tried to call the company, 'tried' as it was either engaged or telling me due to high demand either hang on the phone (55p a minute) or send us an e-mail. Hello, no internet.

Monday 16th July 2014

Joe football.

Shopping.

Got through to the internet company and they said the fault was on my line as their service was working fine. So I rang the telephone company; well, tried. What I've now got is a telephone service that do not answer the phone: I got a machine telling me to do this, do that. Answer the fucking phone, people.

Tuesday 17th July 2014

Woke at half four this morning with a very cheery disposition, gave Joe a kiss as he passed me a cup of tea, then he stands up and said, 'I'm off to pick Chris and the girls up from the airport.' Oh mate. Chris and the girls came straight here, so by seven this morning had Baby who nearly split me eardrums squealing with excitement as she told me how she'd had tea with Mickey Mouse and then swam with da fishes: Sandy had taken Baby and Molly swimming with the dolphins. Chris viewed from a distance: she'd had migraine for two days and after reading that porpoises can detect illness she didn't wanna share the same space as them in case they circled her, just staring at her head, thus confirming that this was no headache but probably a tumour.

Welcome home, Chris. xx

Roll on Wednesday, Penny's birthday going to Cheekz. Gonna need it.

Thursday 19th July 2014

Had my hair done for night out yesterday; getting ready, I was playing some tunes with much complaint from the kids. So I want to clear something up once and for all: disliking a teenager's choice of music has got nothing to do with my age, it's their taste in music is just *shit*. And as for over the hill? I don't remember even climbing one.

Feeling it today after Cheekz: I hurt in places I didn't even know I had. Well worth it. I think.

Saturday 21st July 2014

Edward's 19th birthday.

I had no intention of getting up early today. I was doing that thing where you stretch and roll, pushing your feet into the cold patches, hoping to nod off again. I could hear Joe in the kitchen, vaguely. I heard a kettle whistle; very odd, as ours is electric. And then there was silence, an uncomfortable silence. Oh, how I tried to ignore it, but gave in and got up. As I strolled down the stairs, Joe was glaring at the cat. The cat was purring loudly. Joe was a funny shade of grey. Without diverting his eyes he pointed at his foot. Concertinaed between three toes was a dead mouse. Dead from injury, I'm guessing, as that kettle noise must have been its life essence expelled from its body as 18 stone trod on it. 'As quiet as a mouse', lol. *Not.*

Sunday 22nd July 2014

As Chris was already at the caravan we thought we'd go spend the day with them, so off we went to Leysdown with the grandchildren in tow. We all went crabbing, or as Connor says, 'sabbing'. One bucket full of crabs, six shrimps... and one baby swan, closely followed by its much larger mother. Graceful they may be, but definitely off its nut.
Flying out to New York tomorrow. xx

Thursday 26th July 2014

Arrived New York on the Monday. Chloe and Julie were already at the airport when I got there; Julie had come straight from Paris. Chris rang me at the airport to ask me if it's normal for the membrane covering your eye to move when you push it. That girl needs a life. And I need a new phone number.

Tuesday, we spent a long day shopping in the Big Apple, and the evening brought dinner at the Plaza. Wednesday was Elizabeth's 42nd birthday, so we had dinner at Giovanni's, very posh. My, how the other half live.

Me and Julie got home around five. I'm knackered, so will be having dinner and an early night.

Sunday 29th July 2014

Sam turned eight yesterday so Andy and Jess's house was crawling with delinquents. Funny age, that. Seems a lot of them don't clean their teeth, and then I noticed the worst thing I could have, at the top of my list of pet hates: dirty ear holes! Scummy ears have no place in this family. It doesn't matter where I am, if I see anyone with grubby lug holes I can't talk to them, and depending on the level of gross I've been known to heave. Drives me to madness when I see little kiddies like it; what's the matter with these parents? They make sure the tykes are washed and clothed, but forget to clean the ears. Nobody wants to see ear wax, especially from little kids, the stuff hanging out of theirs is like mud. People with unclean ears defend themselves with the excuse that it's painful and dangerous to poke around in there and it could damage the hearing. Well, aren't these the same people who end up with blocked painful ears, can't hear a thing, then have to have their ears syringed? These are the ones in my mind that are the scum of the earth; anyone who's ears are so full that a doctor has to drain them should be ashamed of themselves.

Monday 30th July 2014

Joe football.

This week's ailment for Chris:forgetful and indecisive. I'm like that all the time, it's called being female.

Wednesday 1st August 2014

Rosie's first birthday.

Because Jessica was getting stuff ready for Rosie's BBQ, me and Joe offered to pick Connor up from Summer Day Camp. Unbeknown to us the police had visited earlier to give them a talk on dangerous drivers, including people who drink and drive. Connor casually told the officer that his granddad does it all the time, and takes a swig when he stops at traffic lights. Oh, it pained me to explain to the teacher that it's bottled water.

Thursday 2nd August 2014

Conifer man.

Was going out this morning then I remembered the 'conifer man' is coming. Why is this important to me?

Saturday 4th August 2014

Poker night.

Felt like a caged animal, so angry at the cast still on my arm, so I thought I'd clear the loft. Mate, the attic is just one big *crap* drawer.

Didn't get very far; become very tearful as I trailed through memories.

Sunday 5th August 2014

Guessing we had Hitchcock-type flock of birds visit the garden: I went out to hang out the washing and noticed Joe's perfectly ripened grapes have been consumed from the vine. Strange I never heard them. Stranger still, Connor never saw them whilst in his sand pit.

Mystery solved. xx

Twenty minutes after grapes vanished, Connor has run past me at 20 mile an hour straight into loo. Judging by the way his legs were only moving from the knees down I'll take a wild stab in the dark that he was said flock of pilfering birds.

Hospital 9am.

Joe football.

Shopping.

Off to hospital to have cast removed. So happy. xx

11am, back from hospital now sporting a bright orange cast, bastard still hasn't healed.

Penny's having a shitter day than me; she got told earlier that Mark's having an affair. We've all had our suspicions that he's at it again; he's got a lot of form, that guy. So now Penny's neighbour has said she's seen a woman going into the house after Penny leaves; she hasn't seen her face, just her hair. What kind of woman is that brazen? Julie? lol xx

Rang the others, and as ever we'll rally round to lift her spirits the best we can with several large bottles of wine and full-on karaoke of 'Sisters Are Doing It For Themselves'. Julie has already phoned her and talked her into going away at the weekend for a pamper. I know she puts up with it, but I still feel sorry for her.

Julie here for dinner.

Got up this morning and right hand looked like an inflated rubber glove. Rushed to the hospital: new cast was too tight. Now sporting a green cast. Someone's having a laugh with me.

Had Penny on the phone in tears: cheering night and pamper weekend are off. Julie had popped in hers on the way to work. After she left, Penny went next door for a coffee

and the neighbour has said that Julie is 'the other woman'.
Julie was clearly pissed off with the accusation so I went
round Penny's to confront the neighbour. She was out, so I
reminded Penny that Julie had dented the woman's car last
year, coupled with her husband always making a bee line to
chat to Julie at Penny's BBQ's: obvious grudge. Two hours
later it's too late for the pamper weekend, but at least the
sisters have kissed and made up. What a bitter old bag she
has living next door.

Wednesday 8th August 2014

Julie got here around seven last night for dinner. No sooner
had we sat down to eat she confessed all: she is the woman the
neighbour saw, she's been knocking Mark off for months. What
do I do? They're both my friends, they're sisters, for Christ's
sake. can't ignore what I've been told: thanx to Julie I'm privy to
the truth. Do I tell Penny? Not tell, and convince Julie to leave
well alone? What? 1st mistake: opening the front door to Julie
2nd mistake: seeking advice from Joe. Sum total of his pearls of
wisdom: 'Slag!'
Definitely touched a nerve when I said maybe best to go with
the 'What you don't know can't hurt you. 'Not the brightest
move on my behalf: Joe's not talking to me. Cheers, Julie. Have
now decided not to tell Penny. Julie gave me her word not to go
there again and telling Penny will only make her existence more
painful. Mark's been having affairs since they met, and she's
vowed she'll never leave him.

Grandkids for dinner.

Why hasn't a can opener been invented that can complete its one and only task from beginning to end, i.e. open a can. It took me five attempts to remove the lid, which in the end I had to bend back, which caused me to slip and saw through (to the bone) four fingers. Now sporting four white plasters. Every time Sam passes by me I get a chorus of 'Billie Jean is not my luvva'.

Hospital 10am.

Leg wax 2pm.

Week 6 enduring cast. Hospital at 10.00 am. Can't take no more, I don't care if it's healed or not, I aint having another cast. I will tell the doctor straight.

12pm. Home, crap home, back from hospital, and yes, got another cast. I told the doc, stood my ground right up to the part he said I could lose my thumb if it doesn't heal right. That was all I needed to know, thank you.

Chloe and Paul arrived at four; tonight we're all going to the dog track.

Julie texted and has just informed me she'll be bringing Gerry to the barbeque tomorrow. I need to tell Joe the situation beforehand, but can't find the words to explain; he's still disgusted with her over the Mark thing, let alone geezer bird.

Saturday 11th August 2014

BBQ 12pm.

Well, that was emotional, having bottled warning Joe and said nothing. Big mistake. Joe and Gerry got on like a house on fire, so well in fact that Gerry jokingly said that Joe was cute enough to convert her. Barbeque abruptly ended when Joe started yelling that he didn't bat for the other side, so I then thought telling him that he was actually a she would somehow show him that it was a compliment, not a gay pick-up line. That went down like a lead balloon. I'm not sure if Joe believes I'm telling him the truth, but either way has vowed that Julie is a seriously messed-up individual.

Monday 13th August 2014

Joe football.

Shopping.

After Paul and Chloe left for home Sunday, me and Chris jumped on a train and took all the kids to Mum's caravan for the day. We took them swimming. The lifeguard was ya usual pratt with an inflated ego: he told the little uns he has to cover the pool at night and if you can run fast enough across it you do what's called the 'Jesus run' on the water's surface. The boys were adamant they were gonna do it before we went home, so I did what all obliging grandmothers do and catered to the ego of the numpty long enough for Connor and Sam to do their thing, for which they seemed grateful. Then Joe arrived to pick us up and they preceded to wind him up with, 'Nan's been flirting with the lifeguard. 'Nothing like thanks. Little shits. xx

Forced Joe to buy a new lawn mower today, couldn't take no more of the sodding dragmo.

Chris now thinks she has a stomach ulcer. Oh. That's the best I can manage right now.

Wednesday 15th August 2014

Hairdresser 5pm.

Chris threw a BBQ for Sandy's birthday yesterday. As usual, Daisy could be found in the possession of chocolate (de-foiled).She stood with chocolate round her mouth and Jessica remarked how grubby she was to which the little angel folds her arms, huffs and declares, 'Mummy, how could I know? My eyes are here'- pointing indignantly -'I can't see my mouth.'

It is Week 9 of incarceration of arm, so long in fact that I have now grown attached to the cast. It doesn't look so pretty as we've been gardening, and had a loft clear out; there's nothing I can't do with it. Joe won't miss it especially at night when I turn over in bed and I clump him in the face. Hmm, gonna miss it more now. Removal tomorrow, 9.30am

Thursday 16th August 2014

Hospital 9.30am cast off, yay. xx

It's *hideous*...It's become a glowing white thing. My arm is skinny, dry and flaky, lol. I shall name it Julie. xx

Plus side I can scratch it without looking over my shoulder

and seeing Joe with a raised eyebrow, tutting. Downside, I've gotta do exercises to rebuild the muscle movement. Other than that, it's all good.

Yes! Freedom. xx

Friday 17th August 2014

Girls' night Tina's.

Julie has set off for a few days at Chloe's. My thoughts are with you, Paul. Better sleep with one eye open, pal.

We had a pleasant but quiet night at Tina's, and with the absence of Julie the subject of marriage rose again. Penny informed us that she's no longer talking to her neighbour and that she and Mark are going to renew their vows. Really wasn't missing Julie at this point, as my toes began to curl.

Realization has just dawned on me that, having purchased another pair of shoes knowing damn well I aint never gonna wear them, I did what seems to be moves executed by an elite commando. Upstairs to the place I squirrel them away, stacked behind my dresses, which seem to have multiplied tenfold.

Saturday 18th August 2014

Diane's baby due.

Joe was breaking up an old wardrobe this afternoon; a piece of wood bent like a boomerang shot off and whipped me across the wrist. I stopped crying after about ten minutes, refused to go to the hospital, hoping it aint broken again. He did say he was sorry. Not very believable when he's doubled over laughing his arse off. Guess revenge really is sweet.

Sunday 19th August 2014

Marie and Leonard's anniversary.

Andy, Jess and the kids came for dinner. To keep the kids amused I set them up outside with a tea set; Daisy and the boys were playing Tea Party in the garden. Having given them 2 litres of cola for pot refills, Daisy all but two minutes later shouts for more drink. A little bewildered that they'd consumed 2 litres already, I shouted out to Connor to see if Daisy had spilt it all. He replied, 'No, Nan, the tea bags drunk it all.' Teabags? Casually I walk out the garden and see tampons swollen and wedged in the cups. All tampons bar one have been removed without too many awkward questions. Notice I said all but one? Connor has drawn eyes on it, named it Lenny and vehemently insists it's a mouse.

Tuesday 21st August 2014

Julie came for dinner last night, and God forbid I asked her how her weekend at Chloe's went. She insists great, and is not waiting for an excuse to go back soon: great house, great food, excellent moonshine, lol, and very friendly locals. It was that last bit that worried me. Apparently farmer Gerry wasn't talking about the ram! Chloe, thinking Julie had gone for a ramble in the hills, was dumbfounded to hear it was more a fumble in the mill, with Gerry. Who, incidentally, is in his 50s, but Julie informs me, 'Sod age, under his Argyll jumper he' s pure prime beef. 'Upside is at least Chloe don't have neighbours, and at least it happened in distant hills. Apparently not, lol: in the hills, yes, and on a haystack, and over a tractor. Chloe was horrified and duly lectured Julie on the risk of his wife finding out, as all the women there are licensed to own guns. Julie assured Chloe that no one was gonna get shot as Gerry had asked if it would be OK if his wife could watch. Mate, she has no shame. For once I agree with Joe: she definitely needs help.

Wednesday 22nd August 2014

Maternity 8pm.

Diane has given birth to a baby boy yesterday, I bestowed upon her the cutest outfit and the font of my advice from experience. *Do not* look at crotch any time soon after having a baby. I will never forget the nasty shock I had seeing a gaping wound that no matter how hard I tried could never imagine would ever return to an acceptable size. Julie asked how much he weighed, followed by 'Is he ugly?' I do wonder if a heart beats in that silicone chest of hers. Still, fair play, we were all thinking it, lol, as the father has the face of a sparrow hawk. Luckily enough he looks like Diane, and as Elizabeth always says 'looks are not everything'. Maybe not, but it does help. She don't give a toss, she's just getting defensive cos she used to go out with the geezer herself, told to me in confidence; shared it with Chloe and Julie immediately, many fits of laughter to date.

Paul invited Gerry and Deidre for dinner. Chloe struggled to look into their faces all evening, then grew really concerned that they seemed really eager to get Paul over to the farm. Chloe having made all sorts of excuses like being busy for next ten years reckoned this seemed to fuel them even more to get Paul to come alone. Julie is receiving all the blame, as Chloe reckon it's Gerry's turn to watch, and thanx to Julie they probably think we're all fair game.

Why, when you've hit your thumb with a hammer, do you not only hit it again in the exact same spot, but hit it twice as hard?

Saturday 25th August 2014

Julie's 39th birthday.

Last night Elizabeth and Chloe arrived here by six. We were at Wheelwrights for dinner then Cheekz. Paul text Chloe to say he'd accepted invite to dinner at Derek's. Chloe still hasn't said anything to Paul about Julie's Highland Fling, as he is on side with Joe and feels disgusted over the whole lesbian thing. She's tried allsorts to discourage Paul from going to Gerry's, but he's clearly not taken the hint. We're all meeting up for lunch today at twelve, then we're having dinner at Tre meur tonight, quite low key, for Julie's birthday. Think she's feeling a bit guilty about Paul. Yeah, right .Oooooh that would knock her ego, Paul never accepting any of Julie's advances over the years, and ending up in the sack with frumpy Deirdre, lol. Ooh, lol. xx

Jessica, knowing she had to go shopping today, has thrown

Lenny the tampon mouse away, with much protesting from Connor, who cannot understand why it's not acceptable to carry Lenny around the supermarket. He demanded '*Why?*' In true parent 'who don't wanna explain' style, she throws him the 'You'll understand when you grow up.'

Poor little sod, how annoying is that answer?

Sunday 26th August 2014

The garden spotlight needed replacing today, despite Joe's track record of luck being zero too none. He was being sensible and removed the fuse for the entire downstairs lighting. I was getting something from the freezer when I could hear what can only be described as wet bacon being thrown into a very hot frying pan. Stumped, I stuck my head out the back door and asked Joe if he'd heard the strange noise. He starts shouting at me, shouting like a madman, 'Answer the phone will ya!' What? Bewildered I said, 'What phone?' At this point he's now screaming at me, 'The fucking phone that's ringing.' Nearly wet myself. It seems in hindsight the garden light is actually wired into the mains via the loft, removal of fuse pointless. So Joe was having several thousand volts shot through his body, lol. Hence the ringing.

Wednesday 29th August 2014

Ian 41st birthday.

Chris now has loss of concentration. So glad I sodded off

Monday to Chloe's for a couple of days with the grandkids. Having now been set free from the 'cast' and aggravated to hell by Julie's affair with Mark, Joe suggested I should get away. I protested vehemently that I have too much to do here, and he assured me he'd fill my shoes and take care of the house. Was not convinced, but really wanted to go.

So I get back from Scotland this morning and, oh, men wonder why they get shouted at. He practically forced me out of my own home on the bullshit promise the house would be cleaned as I would expect. I put my hands up to being a perfectionist, but this was slack, the idea of housework evades him: to him, stacking shit in piles instead of throwing stuff away or returning it to its rightful place, then running a Hoover around, is cleaning. No, mate. I have had to retrace his steps and do it right, and instead of having the brain to keep it shut he opened his gob and said I was picky! Picky, picky, he's a man, he thinks in black and white; me, it's the grey. Dusting, wiping woodwork down, light switches, grill pan, bin tops, actually clean the bathroom which includes pulling *his* hair out the plughole, cleaning the toilet is more than waving the bog brush around the pan. On the promise of ramming the bog brush down his throat if he said another word, he has walked out. Dick.

He's out tonight celebrating his brother's birthday. Bit of luck, he'll stay out.

So short break has caused me grief. And Connor's returned with a phobia. After ignoring repeated warnings not to chase Paul's chickens he blindly ran into the coop and came face to face with the rooster, very big in comparison and not friendly. Fascination with them has gone, as Connor is emotionally scarred for life, lol.

Rhianne 7th birthday.

Hospital 9am.

Daisy won the hearts of the nursing staff when we visited Nan in hospital. Daisy marched up to her bed and shouted, 'Granma, have you misplaced your hip?'After suffering the geriatric ward for half an hour, which was at least 27 minutes more than I could handle, me and madam popped into town and bought Rhianne a cup cake maker. Very girlie, very pink. No good for my granddaughter. xx

Sunday 2nd September 2014

Went uniform shopping with Jessica on Friday. I was explaining how I've always pondered as to why some kids wear shoes too big for them. We were in Farnham's, the only shop you can purchase the uniforms from, and the owner who had heard me goes on to explain that some parents buy the entire uniform including the shoes in the largest sizes regardless of the fit so that the child doesn't out grow it, so the uniform will last them for the entire time they're at school, three years on average. Seriously, what these parents are saving in money the kids are losing in self-esteem.

Popped round Aunt Shirley's with the kids yesterday. On entering the lounge where her beloved cockatiel sits in his cage, Connor marched up to it with a face like thunder, points and says, 'Is that a shicken?'

Joe football.

Shopping.

The doctor has told Chris she's paranoid and that nobody is probably talking behind her back. Oh dear, lol. xx

Car service 9am.

Joe has questioned his recent weight gain, bless him. Phoned me earlier, saying, 'Can you please come out the front of the house and help me out the car?' I ran out in a panic and there sat on the driveway was the smallest courtesy car I've ever seen, and wedged behind the steering wheel sat Joe, looking very pissed off.

Did the school run and popped in Mum's, and Uncle Geoff was there. Connor asked him how old he was. Geoff, a spritely 94, said with a wink that he couldn't remember. So Connor told him to look at the label in his pants as his say '5/6 years'.

Thursday 6th September 2014

Joe dentist 6pm.

Spent a much-needed relaxing evening round Julie's tonight. What I didn't know was Jessica had popped round mine, found I was out and noticed I had washing in the machine, and kindly hung it out. I nearly died when on my return this evening there hanging on my line was under-crackers. This was and is one of the 'never do's' ingrained in me, handed down from generations of matriarchs. You'd be forgiven for murder than to be seen with your smalls out for all and sundry to be viewing.

Saturday 8th September 2014

Paul's 38th birthday.

Paul arrived here Friday around six, and by seven the boys were all gone, to a boxing match. We were all round Abigail's, opted for takeaway after we were offered mung beans and an assortment of nuts.

Tonight sees the boys at the inevitable Flannigan's, which is handy as I've got shitloads to get ready for tomorrow's BBQ.

Monday 10th September 2014

Paul left early for Scotland yesterday. Me and Chris went to Sunday market. By the time we got back Joe already had the BBQ going. I was in the kitchen when Connor flew through the door screeching, 'Nanny, there's a shicken in the garden!'Walking with him hanging off my leg I proceeded to the garden to see a crow devouring the hot dog Connor had lobbed at its head on his hasty departure.

Joe says Julie's like burnt toast: brunette on the outside and blonde in the middle.

Joe told me he's having the day off tomorrow, wants to sort out the conifers. I reminded him that we pay someone for that and he said, 'Yeah, and he's doing a shit job of it. 'Shook me a little: has someone said something? All I did was watch him. Bloody hell. xx

Tuesday 11th September 2014

Before long Accident and Emergency will be naming a wing after us, as we have again spent the day there today. It seems I was innocent after all: Joe hadn't got rid of the conifer guy because of jealousy, it's a lot simpler. Joe being tighter than a duck's arse refused to pay £40 to trim the trees, felt that was a bit steep. So set up the stepladder and climbed from that into the trees: 18 stone man (says he isn't) trying to walk on feeble decaying branches was always gonna spell danger. There was a crack and Joe swiftly vanished from view, having shot downwards screaming (denied vehemently).A rogue stick had wedged itself up his trouser leg and stuck into his flesh. I had to saw him out. All the time wary of the glances over the fence from neighbours, confused as to why I'm sawing like a madman with tears streaming down my cheeks, and the foulest language emanating from the shuddering foliage. Six stitches and £40 later all is as it should be. Thus clearly proving if it has tyres or testicles you're gonna have trouble with it.

Daisy's 3rd birthday.

Got to be at Andy's for four, for Daisy's party, which gave me plenty of time to get to the library as Sam has decided he is now a vegetarian. So that's where I spent my afternoon, consulting the many varieties of vegetarianism. Left having given myself brain ache. I arrived at the party armed with pages of notes and began bleating off the different varieties so I could establish which type Sam was. He just rolled his eyes at me and said, 'Nan, if it's got a face I aint eating it.'

Joe stitches out 10am.

Girls' night here.

Mum rang earlier from the caravan. The call lasted about an hour; think it was to release tension as she knew Chris was on the way for the weekend. Joe kept huffing and looking at the clock, which was annoying. It's no secret I can talk on the phone for hours: what woman can't? We cover anything to everyone, and this eludes Joe. For him a call is, 'Hello. Yeah. OK. Better go, see ya.' To him, if someone calls with a question, answer it and ta ra. Der... it's called a conversation. Piss off moaning about me, Billy No Mates.

Bread, *seriously*! You remove it from the packet, check it all over and spy not a speck of blue in sight, give it a good sniff, perfect. Make the sarnie, and as soon as you've finished eating the first half your taste buds are engulfed in the essence of *dirt* with a dewy hue. You feel you must have missed something that only a microscope could have detected, but yet on turning over the remaining half the entire thing is aquamarine. WTF? Does it react with the atmosphere, or what?

Teacher Training Day.

Teacher Training Day today, which means the kids are off school, so we thought it'd be fun to take them to the forest. *Do not think* for one minute that anything you've ever told kids sinks in. A lovely serene day in the forest quickly turned to hell as Sam, unbeknown to any of us, had spotted and retrieved a leather bag from the reeds at the side of the river. In what was like a scene from *Chariots of Fire* I ran for what seemed a very slow lifetime towards Sam, shouting, 'Noo, don't open it!' Too late. As I skidded to a halt crashing into a wall of stench I spied through the open zipper what I suspected it was gonna be: a dead cat. Sam's nostrils expanded by a foot as he caught the full waft, then heaved his guts up. Daisy started crying, and everyone passing the once beautiful spot kept checking the soles of their shoes, soon realising what it was, shouted over, 'Ooh, you didn't wanna be looking in that. 'No shit, Sherlock. We quickly found the park keeper, gave him the bag and scuttled off. The car was parked half a mile away and I could still smell death as we drove off.

Chris said she keeps napping. The doctor was fool enough to say perhaps your blood sugar is low; she now believes she must be borderline diabetic.

Tuesday 18th September 2014

Shopping.

Another thing about telephones – and this is mainly a male crime – is I've noticed 'the telephone voice'. Why do people feel they have to speak in a creepy, almost apologetic tone? I don't do it. Weirdo's.

Chris was at the docs again today. Threw me a bit: thought I'd lost a day. Her headache is back and, given the recent other stuff, she thinks her tumour has grown.

Tony, cooking tomato soup, knocks the pan over, tipping the rather warm substance which lands on the cat from the waist down. The cat immediately straightens its legs out in front of itself and glides at rapid speed around the carpet like a hovercraft, lol. This is why I have so many pairs of knickers, ha hee.

Thursday 20th September 2014

Why is it that when cracks appear in a marriage, women will always attempt to talk to the husband, but because it's more the way you're feeling rather than thinking, you have to try and explain it the best way possible. Admittedly, in a man's defence, it does come out all confusing, but instead of tuning in and listening properly he will just say, 'So you want to leave, then.' See, it's that male black and white thinking again - black or white stay or go - instead of our grey area that means, 'I want to stay but things need sorting out.'

This ignorance doesn't just apply to their spouse, they exhibit it toward the kids as well. For example, if one of them has sneaked a couple of quid out your purse, without question he will flip his lid, call them thieving bastards, verbally beat them down for hours. Whereas a female will more than likely have a go at them but will stop and ask why, as there may have been an underlying reason that caused them to steal from you. Must be very simple in a man's head.

Saturday 22nd September 2014

Leg wax 2pm.

Attended the traditional Harvest Festival at Sam's school yesterday and noticed that the legendary 'fringe by Mum 'still lives on! Cut 3 inches above the eyebrows; not a good look in any decade. I wonder if this crime is committed by the same mothers who buy the school uniform that lasts three years? Do they think they'll grow into the fringe? pml, xx

Cooker died last night, have ordered a new one. I've been assured new one will be delivered and fitted in two days. Call me cynical, but having paid for express delivery, like a fool, I know I'm living in false hope that it actually means something.

Sunday 23rd September 2014

Me and Joe were playing on the floor with Daisy. She wanted a drink so I reached out my arms and told her to help me up. Having risen with ease to a standing position Joe reached out, calling rather pathetically, 'What about me?', to which she answered with a sigh, 'I can't, Granddad, you're too fat.' Mate, killed by a three-year-old.

Joe's really not having a good day, he just had the fright of his life, lol, pml. We were discussing the legendary 'bogey man 'and we both agreed that no parent we've ever heard of has ever told a child that the bogey man will get you on the stairs, either chasing you up or on your way down. Yet we all believe that no sooner does your foot touch the first step than the hair on your neck stands up and the countdown begins, giving us ten seconds – no more, no less – to reach either the top or the bottom. Having had the kids round earlier we'd put up the stair gate. As we ascended the stairs for bed, Joe lifted the gate to bring it up, without his knowledge the middle section was unlocked and swung inwards, and the cold hard metal pushed into his lower back, he screamed (says he didn't) then exhaled a ooh with a clear look of fear in his eyes. Oh, how I'm laughing right now. If looks could kill… He said it was a heart-stopper as it had felt like an icy finger poking him, lol. Don't matter how old we get, we clearly still need to leg it on the staircase.

Monday 24th September 2014

Joe football.
Shopping.
Could clearly sense Joe's apprehension on the stairs tonight,

especially when I'm sure I heard him counting. I was only halfway up when I thought I heard him mumble 'Six' behind me, which was followed closely by, 'Hurry up, for fuck's sake.' Oh dear I shall surely laugh myself to death. Bless him, may fold under questioning. xx

Tuesday 25th September 2014

How disgusting is peanut butter? Peanuts smell like old farts at the best of times, but then it's mixed to a texture of shit. Not a fan, lol.

Wednesday 26th September 2014

Mutley vets 10am.
Love bites: how cool do youngsters think they are when they parade theirs about? Shows the extent of their self-respect, does it not? Bit harsh: we've all been there, lol. The ones that are repulsive have got to be the 30-plus group: grow up, for fuck's sake.

Thursday 27th September 2014

George 71st birthday.
Window cleaner.
Prostitution is probably the oldest occupation and still the

most frowned-upon profession. The way I see it, it's obviously here to stay, so let's help them out. Legalise it, give them somewhere safe to work, with security and health screening. Let them provide the service safely; they're gonna anyway. You see, all the ones against them who think they're depraved individuals who are the scourge of society are very naive. These people should open their eyes to a few facts: most prostitutes are not performing sadistic, depraved sexual favours for these men that we ourselves wouldn't take part in at home, it's usually a lot more basic than that.

Mate, I'm sympathising with prostitutes now; what's going on with me?

Friday 28th September 2014

Girls' night Abigail's.

Men and women should *never* go shopping together, seriously Joe!'Why would you need another pair of shoes? You clearly have years left in your others.' Not need, pal, *want*. Quite funny really, seeing as its most of us wives that buy the old man's clothing, which means his wardrobe is bulging and so is his shoe cupboard with his ten pairs of boots, barely worn, and six different pairs of trainers. Bloody hypocrite.

Saturday 29th September 2014

No sign of the gas engineer yet but the new cooker has turned up today, hooray! Now all we need to do is get it fitted and put the kitchen back together.

Joe football.

Working down mines sixty hours a week, laying railroads across deserts? Not a touch on the stress and physical exhaustion inflicted by trying to dress a one-year-old into a snowsuit. When or even if you get one foot in, it's accompanied by the lining of the leg hanging out the end. After much scraping, tugging and rolling the poor girl this way and that, sweating enough to fry chips, you eventually get the arms in. More pulling is required as now the slippery lining is seeping from every cuff, causing the poor little bugger to stoop like a hunchback. By now Rosie has had enough and is refusing to go in the buggy. She starts imitating a cat that don't wanna be put into a box: frozen star jump, head thrown back. I now have to force the demon down with one knee across her lap, simultaneously prising both hands from the sides, and at the speed of light put together and clip the harness, trapping the skin of two fingers. This could be an Olympic sport; not for the faint-hearted, it's a cross between a marathon and going ten rounds with Stone Cold Steve Austin. Incidentally, the latter I'd love to do.

Shopping.

Apparently some men do clean and tidy, not only to a woman's standard but even further; so extreme that in fact the house is no longer a home but a show house. Lies.

Had a spiffing afternoon. Chris had to go to hospital and have a camera up her arse and down the throat; can only presume they wiped it after the first one, lol. The official results will be at our doctors in a week but the consultant who performed the procedure said from what he could see there was nothing to worry about. He did say to Chris there was a lot of faeces in the bowel and said she should eat more fibre. He's got seven years at medical school and a degree to point out what we all knew, which is that Chris is full of shit.

Saturday 6th October 2014

Poker night.

Shopping.

Friday morning I had to take Chris shopping for fibrous foods, as I knew in my heart we'd find her sprinkling bits of wool on her dinner. Cannot remember much about Penny's last night: as Chris began the blow-by-blow details of her endoscopic adventure I rapidly consumed a bottle of wine, vaguely hearing the sounds of 'Errgh 'followed by gagging, until I happily lost the ability to speak and Joe came and got me.

Arhh! *Men.* Why do they constantly go on about all the 'unnecessary extras' we're putting in the trolley whenever we go shopping? No matter how many times I say 'The kids might like it' or 'It might be nice to try something different', I always have to listen to him moaning and huffing. Yet I can guarantee Joe will be the first in the fridge later, Greeding it all.

Tramps: every borough has one, everybody knows them by name – usually George. Apart from the similarities shared by all, i.e. obvious wafts of pissy drawers and dirt, they all have a limp. I'm not talking about the type me and Julie had a run in with, technically they're not tramps, just piss heads. So I was saddened to hear that our local tramp was found murdered. How low do you have to be?

Soon dragged back into the real world: Chris, Monday, doctors. The back pain she keeps getting has somehow convinced her that whatever was in her stomach has now spread to her spine. Lol, she don't have one.

Small consolation: it's Abigail's 44th birthday tomorrow, she's having a BBQ. Virgil! Mate, bloody hell.

Hairdresser 5pm.

Book another blood test.

Managed to avoid any direct conversation with Virgil last night.

Receptionists! Not office girls, but the miserable bastards that work at doctors surgeries or hospitals. Who the hell do these women think they are? Whatever need for treatment is never good enough in their eyes. I rang the surgery was greeted with a 'What do you want?' tone. Der, to see a doctor. It's bad enough trying tell me there's no available appointments for the next five years, until insisted, when she followed up with, 'Oh,I can fit you in. 'As if this hadn't narked me enough she uttered the immortal words, 'What is it for?'Somebody please explain why patient confidentiality is paramount in their job. Why, then, are these positions held by nosey bastards? I replied, 'Are you a qualified GP?''What's that?''No? Then mind your own business.'

Having got an appointment for ten, I arrived at the surgery and I can see her putting my face to the voice on the phone earlier. She gives me a snotty sneer from behind her counter, blatantly ignores me, pretending to type on her keyboard, then took another call.,Mate,how I resisted the urge not to reach over the counter and wipe the smug look off her face. Stopped only by the strategically placed sign warning that 'Violence towards members of staff will not be tolerated and you will be prosecuted'. Gonna be honest, I did ponder what the charge would be for one quick smack in the mouth.

Hospital A&E are the best place to find the worst form of these birds. I can understand that some days must be really busy, and yes, maybe a lot of casualties have self-inflicted injuries through nothing more than their own stupidity, but again, what the hell has it got to do with these women? How busy can the job really get? They sit on their arse tapping info into a computer, then tell you to follow a coloured line on the floor. They work in a hospital, for fuck's sake: what did they expect, that no one would be ignorant enough to turn up and want to be treated? They don't intimidate or impress me, but I've witnessed them have such a belittling effect on some people they've practically apologised for needing medical assistance. This being the reason I behaved myself at the doctors this morning.

The day that Sam fell out the tree and put his teeth through his lip, all of us rushed to the hospital. Both Sam and Jessica were covered in blood, crying, others in the queue ushered them to the front where the receptionist looked Jess up and down and in a snide tone said, 'Hmm, how did this happen?'I quickly took over ushering Jess to the first doctor I saw walk past, went back to the desk and gave her something to think about, much to the cheers of everyone else. This is why they get verbally abused, and sometimes assaulted.

Thursday 11th October 2014

It's that dreaded time of year tomorrow. Birthday! Joe buying gifts, ha ha. I live in dread. He's one of them, even if I say out loud. 'That dress in the window's nice but I wouldn't wear it' makes perfect sense in any language; not to a bloke it don't. He *will* go and buy it and then stand there dumbfounded while I'm sneering at him. He'll ask me what I want for my birthday, and whatever I say he ignores. This year if he does it I'm gonna snap. I am no longer giving a shit about hurting his feelings. Brutal, but it's better than having to keep lying that said garment is in the wash or, worse still, actually have to wear it at some time to keep the charade going. No more wearing perfume that smells like Liberace's pant drawer, or shoes his Nan would be comfortable in. Sod him. He should know me well enough by now to know what I would and wouldn't wear; failing that, at least have the decency to listen to what I say.

Friday 12th October 2014

41stbirthday.

Un-fucking believable! A leather jacket with 'Harley' emblazoned across the back. Yes, I flipped. Yes, I was nasty. Yes, he stormed out somewhere and the kids have all got the hump with me. Because it was 'bang out of order', out of bloody order, *out of bloody order!* What someone should be saying is, 'Who the fuck was he thinking about when he bought it?' Followed by, 'Has he got a bird on the side and is she a butch biker?' He returned an hour later with flowers. Mate: horse and bolted. Was feeling a slight pang of guilt when he says he'd taken his brother with him when he bought it and Ian had said, 'D'ya know what you're doing? The Debbie I know would not wear that ever.' He's gone again, good fucking riddance. Dickhead. We're supposed to be going to Penny and Mark's renewal tomorrow. What a joke, wouldn't marry Joe again.

Sunday 14th October 2014

Penny and Mark renewal 3pm Country Club.

Remained in a foul mood Saturday and still not talking to Joe even today. Penny and Mark seemed to have a good day if you can ignore that it's a crock. If he didn't take the first vows seriously, what makes her think renewing them will? It's said that your average white wedding cost £21,000 and I reckon yesterday cost at least half that amount, and there was Penny and Mark who spent the entire evening going from one relative to another not knowing who the hell some of them were. By the time they'd finished the party was over and all they got for their money was one glass of champagne and a dance. How do unremembered relatives get invited? His mother: lol, it's the classic 'If you invite so and so you have to invite him or her because she'll tell so and so and he or she will feel offended, blah blah blah.' Why worry? You're never gonna see these people again unless there's another wedding or a death, so why give a toss about upsetting someone?

This is what truly causes all the stress associated with wedding planning, not the outfits, flowers or the catering, but the invite list. No matter what you decide, someone is not going to be happy. If it's low budget you can't afford to have every guest at the sit-down meal so you put them on the evening list, which then screams you've got favourites. Who sits where? You never hear of arrangements being awkward because everyone wants to be near someone particular. Nope, always it's you can't sit so and so next to him or her or there'll be murder. These are always the people you neither know, like nor want that are controlling your big day. Why is there a head table? So's you can sit there with the people you love in this life and the rest can sod off.

Avoiding some like the plague, you always get caught by the odd one: 'I haven't seen you in years!' That was the plan. 'How long's it been?' Not long enough. 'What are you doing with yourself?' Trying to think of an excuse to get away from you. Such bullshit. Wouldn't it be much more fun if everyone was honest? 'How have you been?' Fine until I saw you. 'Christ, haven't you grown?' Oh, did you think I was still gonna be ten? Moron. 'It's nice all of us back together. 'Truth. The only reason these relatives have turned up is for free booze and grub; the best deterrent is to write at the bottom of the invite, 'There is not a free bar'. These people will decline and remark they never expected you to pay for drinks at their do, forgetting that they never even invited you. Funerals have to be the biggest of their frauds: 'I've come to pay my respects. 'Most weren't respectful in life, why now? Guilty conscience, maybe? Might be in the will? Failing that, it'll be the free booze and grub again. Parties held at home tend to keep the arseholes away; obnoxious relatives don't seem to be brave enough to test your politeness and control when you're on your own turf.

Got back from the Sunday market and Joe has cleaned the entire house and cooked dinner. Still angry as hell, but I'm acting like I'm not

Joe football.

Shopping.

Came through the door yesterday having bought the boys new jackets. Thought Joe was gonna have a moan but even I credit him with enough brain not to as no, they didn't need them, but I wanted to get them: who could resist three-quarter length leather jackets? Pricy, but they'll look after them. Must remember to tell Sam it's fake leather. Not sure if real hide is a problem now he's a vegetarian. This morning, however, it seems Joe's found his voice again giving it the 'Err, the boys are only eight and five, you tell yourself they'll look after them if you must, luv.' Dick. xx

Was telling Chris, when she pipes up, 'He's got a point: how many coats can two small humans need?'

Bitch. Seriously? *Want* not needs. Who do they think they are, my muvva?

Schools shut as they have no heating, so we decided to take the kids to Southend for the day. Weather was crap, gale warnings were issued and torrential rain all day. It wasn't much fun for Sam and Connor so when they asked if they could walk on the beach and throw skimmers, I let them, warning them both not to get their shoes wet. We averted our eyes for a millisecond and both the boys were in the sea up to their necks, in their new coats, and yet placed carefully on the sand were two pairs of shoes. Cringed as I saw Joe's lips start to move, 'What did I tell you. 'My only defence, rather pathetic, was I hadn't been specific enough about apparel. That failed so I told him they'd obviously inherited his div gene.

Wednesday 17th October 2014

Joe picking Daisy up from nursery.

Daisy presented Joe with a lovely painting of an octopus which in her words has 'eight testicles'. Equalled only by the time that her dad, aged three, told my mum that a dolphin is a big fish with an arsehole on its head.

Thursday 18th October 2014

Went round to see Connor earlier as he's not feeling very well. He needed another dose of medicine and tried to undo the cap himself and couldn't. I explained to him that it's a childproof lid. He stared at me, then the bottle, and said, 'Nan, how does it know it's me?'

Sunday 21st October 2014

Jeni and Jaki turned eighteen yesterday. Chloe's in Los Angeles with them. Girls' night was held at Chris's which went pleasantly well, no whining or self-diagnosis. So well in fact when she said she was going Mum's caravan Saturday, I agreed we'd join her for the day as we were babysitting anyway.

Two good days out of three is better than the average in this family, got up this morning and thanks to Mr Helpy Helper I've had to call Gina and have my eyebrows reshaped and coloured. My lighter had run out so I'd put it in the crap drawer for refilling (that never happens) and unbeknown to me Joe *has* refilled it, last night. Forgetting why it was in the crap drawer and not knowing anything of the above, I held the lighter as close to my fag as possible, cos every smoker knows if and only if it has a scrap of life left in it the flame will be almost invisible and will extinguish fast. Bit of a shock as I was greeted by a wall of bright orange flame and a funny smell. Lucky I have a face, let alone dodgy brows and stubby eyelashes, but on the upside I no longer have the makings of a moustache. To think I had to marry Joe to find out how divvy he is. Then again I should have guessed that when he asked me to marry him, lol.

Monday 22nd October 2014

Joe football.

Doctor reckons Chris has got 'irritable bowel', lol. More like irritating bastard.

Think this MLC malarkey is starting to make some sense: the first half of our life is for others and the second half is for oneself. Must have missed something.

Academic Tutor Day 10am.

Hmm, payback is a bitch. Joe was coming with me to the school today and when I got in the passenger seat I noticed it was right back. Being only 5 foot tall I know I'd never have moved it. I jokingly said, 'You had your bird in here.' Without a snicker he said, 'Sorry, luv, she's got very long legs.' Shame on me. Definitely knows what I said about conifer man.

Thursday 25th October 2014

Elizabeth and Chloe arrive London.

A little faith has been restored in sons: Tony didn't like the long-legged bird joke by his dad so he hid in the airing cupboard with a balloon, and as Joe passed he let the air out through the crack of the door. He screamed, no matter what he says.

Saturday 27th October 2014

Zero's fancy dress last night, good night. xx

Elizabeth is doing some shopping up the West End before heading home; Chloe already gone. It's been four weeks since the delivery of the new cooker; at last the engineer had put in an appearance. He titted around for two hours, says 'All done, I'm off.' I looked at the cooker and it's as bent as a nine bob note. I've contacted the suppliers and they've assured me a replacement and the engineer will be here in three days, lol. So not gonna be here.

Sunday 28th October 2014

I got a call out of the blue this morning: Anne-Marie, married to Tony, childhood sweethearts, married forever. She's filed for divorce as he's been seeing the woman who does the wages at his garage. Someone tipped her off by putting a note through her door. She's confronted him and he says it's only happened twice: lol, 'only'. Tony being Mark's brother, it clearly runs in the family. She reckons it's been going on for months: he's been distant, exhausted and defensive for ages. They do say hindsight is a bitch. Realising the 'twice' wasn't getting him anywhere he's gone for the classic 'stressed and had needs'. Pathetic, as she only gave birth four months ago to the youngest of four. Threw in the complaint that she's always tired and has left him feeling unloved, aww. Maybe if he'd helped her around the house a bit she'd have been less knackered, leaving some quality time together. He obviously has time enough to spare, shagging the moose from work.

I'm sure someone once said that marital affairs are not always a sign of a troubled marriage. Maybe not, when it's a secret, but it's gonna be when your found out. Who said this? Bet it was a man. Experience shows us that affairs are not only hurtful, they make the whole situation 50 times worse. Christ isn't it bad enough to find out your other half don't want you no more? But to find its cos they want someone else is devastating. If they don't wanna be with you anymore, why don't they just leave? The knife is going to go in deep enough, they don't have to twist it as well.

What we didn't know is this is the second time Tony has done this. She said the first time he convinced her it was 'just a bad patch'. Bullshit, it's called having your cake and eating it. Tony has never once sat Anna-Marie down and said he thought they had marital problems, never even tried to alert her to the fact that he was unhappy. He said that he'd been too afraid to talk to her, tell her how he was feeling, as it would have hurt her. What a crock. Blamed in on the new business, left him feeling he was failing her financially, emotionally and sexually. Leaving because you're unhappy is understandable, and better for both parties rather than get caught in a dirty affair, thus not only hurting your partner as their world falls in on them but they've also been humiliated. (1)He was failing her.(2)When the truth came out he should have been afraid. But Anne-Marie let him off, leaving because he was unhappy is better for both parties, rather than sneaking about with the fear of being caught. Of course this means you're still going to get hurt: not only has your world just fallen on you, he's humiliated you as well.

From a self-confessed sluts point of view, Julie states it's the sneaking around that makes it exciting. fair comment, and for a woman who still has the body of a twenty-something it's easy to get your kit off and roll about in the hay. But I'm sure for the average Joe who's been married for years has stretch marks and hanging flab it must take a lot to push past the boundaries of right and wrong and self-consciousness to have unbridled sex with someone new. If the same effort was directed towards their spouses, maybe the stale marriage would be reignited and there'd be smiles all round. Julie defended herself with the 'Bloody cheek, I have this body cos I am twenty-something', lol. Julie, that might work on the guys she picks up in bars, but this is me she's talking to.

Selfishness is the key here: when cheaters are found out they have only two choices: leave or stay. It's less simple for the innocent partner on the receiving end: if they leave they look like the bad guy, having to walk out the door with confused kids screaming for them to stay, made worse by the fact you'd only be leaving because the shock and distress if you stay make you feel cheap and crap, and you will probably punch the cheating other half in the head, smash the house up, again upsetting the kids.

Jenna tried to justify her decision to let him stay with 'We are rebuilding our relationship, we're gonna work through the problems and feel the affair will make us stronger. 'Is she for real? Rebuilding? Up until Mick's confession, she didn't even know the marriage was broken. Working through our problems? In other words, he's feeling guilty after he realised the grass was not greener. Has made us stronger? Who was she trying to convince, us or herself? What Mick did was *wrong*. He valued his marriage very little, so *why*? Has he come back to flog a dead horse?

Maybe I'm being a little harsh? Hmm, no, if it was you who had had the fling because you felt neglected in the bedroom, would he want you back? If he did, the chances are your sex life will not be neglected but non-existent, cos he wouldn't touch you with a dirty one let alone a clean one. If you left because you'd felt tied down, lacked freedom, is he ever gonna trust you to go out on your own again? Saddest people in these situations has got to be the mistresses: they really seem to fall for the 'My wife doesn't understand me', 'She's a right cow', and let's not forget the 'We sleep in separate beds', the marriage was dead long before meeting her, and the everlasting 'I'm staying for the children'. Okey dokey, then.(1)No doubt some wives are right cows, in truth most are loyal loving women who get the shit end of a deal, does the mistress know her that well? No? Then don't make assumptions. And if indeed you do know her, then who's the real cow? (2)Separate beds, lol, oh ha ha.(3) Staying for the children? Oh grow up, luv! If two people are that attracted to each other and fall in love, right or wrong, nothing, not even a spouse at home, will keep them apart. If you think you mean that much to the guy and are not just a

167

'bunk up', ask yourself why he doesn't have the time to take you out for the evening but yet still attends functions with his wife. Pleads poverty, don't buy you gifts but can still afford to take his family on expensive holidays abroad. Gives you all the excuses of stress and tiredness but on his fleeting visits will always spare enough time for you to fulfil his sexual urges. Julie used to get pressies and romantic weekends out of hers: in honesty says it was because her cheating bastard had more to lose if she'd got pissed off and had gone banging on his door. Plus he was an arrogant, balding, overweight, semi-impotent pratt whose ego trip was worth every penny to spend time with a girl as hot as Julie, cos he knew without flashing the cash she wouldn't have been seen dead with him. Personally, as a self-confessed gold-digger, I think Julie earned every penny, cos from where I'm sitting there's not enough money for me to have sex with a decrepit old man. Like Julie said, that's why she's on 75k a year and we are not. xx

However, some mistresses do bag their bit on the side, even marry them. What the mistress wants to ask is, how did she really get him? Did he really follow his heart or did his wife twig and throw his sorry arse out? Did he really choose you over his wife, or did he need somewhere to stay? Are you so different from his wife that the better woman won, or are you the version that his wife used to be? It's true that most mistresses bear resemblance to the wives, basically just the younger version without the nagging and the kids. Now you've married him you'll soon become the next nagging wife, and he'll be cheating on you. You should know he's already proven he's unfaithful and a quitter; or did you think you were so special he won't do it to you? You're at a worse disadvantage: his ex-wife never doubted his loyalty until she found out about you, whereas you have known from day one what he's capable of. Good luck: what goes around, comes around.

Julie says the secret to being the 'bit on the side' is don't kid yourself that it's anything more than a leg-over with perks. Don't sit in waiting for him to fit you in between his wife and the barmaid from his local, live your life and never be stupid enough to expect the sympathy vote for the way you allow him to make you feel.

Wednesday 31st October 2014

Halloween, taking kids trick or treating.

Bit boring, I opted to be a witch (I could get more clothing under me dress).Joe went as batman from the 70s.

This has to have been one of the funniest nights of my life, as always our street takes Halloween very seriously for the kids and all the houses were decorated to the highest standard. Especially the Richardson's': this year Jamie and Lisa incorporated the garage and Jamie had built a cage which had a live werewolf in it, rattling the metal bars ferociously as the kids approached. Daisy was a bit apprehensive so Joe puffed out his chest, took her hand, laughing and telling her there's nothing to be afraid of, standing 2 foot from the cage as the creature snarled, clawed and rattled the bars. What Joe didn't know was that some of the bars were actually rubber and as he mocked and jeered, the wolf whipped out through the bendy bars and was in Joe's face. He let out such a scream that he startled the wolf, who turned to run and went face first into the metal bars, stiffened and fell on the floor. Through my tears all I could see was the fluttering of a blue cape as it ran down the driveway.

The kids, although startled, were fine when they heard raucous laughter coming from the wolf. Apart from the pain in his side, Jamie was fine, just a little stunned. Was a bit of an awkward silence when we got back to ours: Joe was in the kitchen glass of brandy in his shaking hand and a ladder in his tights. Tony patted him on the shoulder and said, 'You OK nowwo wow oww?'

Sunday 4th November 2014

Spent Friday afternoon shopping for Bonfire Night. Joe bought a ton of fireworks, I left him setting up the garden for the display of the century and buggered off round Tina's for girls' night, having paused to think whether or not I should tell them about Halloween, as it's taken Joe two days to calm down and stop referring to Jamie as 'fucking idiot'. Pause passed, and we proceeded to laugh for an hour or so; the more we drank the more someone texted him asking Joe, 'What's the time?'

Saturday we had a full house for Bonfire Night and Joe showed he'd reached a new level of miser when it turns out the reason he'd bought so many fireworks was they were knocked off and cheap. He nearly killed us all: four exploded, taking out several stone planters; one blew a hole in the lawn; three went up a foot and half in the air, turned horizontal and just missed the little ones. At which point Mutley runs over to a newly lit rocket, grabs it in his teeth, runs around with it in his mouth, then legs it into the house. Luckily they were so crap it burned itself out before blowing the dog's head off.

Chris has gone to the Sunday market with Tina. I couldn't be asked.

Tuesday 6th November 2014

Teacher Training Day.

Note to self: Explain more clearly to a three-year-old what playing Pooh Sticks actually is, lol. xx

Teacher Training Day, so Joe took the day off work and we thought we'd take the kids to the forest, feeling quite confident that no one would be retrieving any abandoned bags. Joe was not impressed as he was standing on the bridge, twig in hand ready to be thrown when a turd hits him in the head. With it still stuck in his hair he turns round and Daisy shouts 'Granddad, yes it does!'

Wednesday 7th November 2014

Violet's 52nd birthday.

Julie and Penny are both having dinner at their mum's for her birthday; let's hope all goes well.

One of Tony's mates was getting a bit lippy earlier and I told him if I was his mother I'd slap him in the mouth. He laughed and said, 'Well, you're old enough to be.'

Saturday 10th November 2014

Poker night.

The cat (clearly Joe's pet as they have the same amount of brain cells) has again brought back another fish from the neighbour's pond; purring and strutting with a cheeky 'Oh look how clever I am' look in his eyes. If only he was the courageous hunter, if only the furry bearer of gifts. Nah, it's the pond weed he likes to collect, that's my reward for his upkeep. As for the fish, they're accidently tangled up in it when he pilfers it from the ponds.

Monday 12th November 2014

Joe football.

Following the substantial snowfall on Saturday night, Sam and Connor were in the garden yesterday making a snow hoe! Stifled a snicker and duly bollocked Tony. Connor was using a rake to accumulate a good supply for Sam, who I myself thought was quite ingenious; Grandpa Grump did nothing but moan at them to be sure to put the rake away when they'd finished, as tools aint cheap.

Thursday 15th November 2014

Hairdresser 5pm.

Had to trundle round the hairdressers tonight as she didn't want to drive in the snow. She may only be five streets away but I'm knackered; my legs are killing me as you cannot walk normally in snow, you have to shuffle like an old fart.

Was watching a documentary on the police force tonight and my heart goes out to them: shit job, the money's nothing special and the risks and dangers are worse than ever. They put their lives in danger to catch the offenders, only then to be sued for doing their job, then the lawyers, judges and outdated laws fail to administer the adequate punishment, if any.

Jackie 25th birthday.

Dinner at Chris's 7pm.

Week 7, two bent cookers, and now the supplier has sent an engineer round with replacement number three: a shiny aluminium hob. Er, hello! All my appliances are white; that is why I bought the new hob in white, people. I advised him as politely as possible that it would be good if he got out my house ASAP as I was going to punch him after he says, 'I'm here now, I could fit it anyway, what's in a colour?'

After yet more snow falling heavily yesterday Joe thought he'd have a relaxing day off today. Seeing that the garden was covered by about 8 inches of snow he thought he'd better go check on the pond. I watched from the warmth of the kitchen as he slowly eased his way across where the path should be, knowing I'm waiting for him to slip arse over tit. Giving me a smug grin accompanied by the bird, he turned, took two-steps, suddenly stood bolt upright then dropped to his knees. No sooner had I slid open the patio door than he turned and scowled at me and I could see blood running through the fingers of his left hand which was covering his nose, and in his right was the rake.

I was ear-wigging at the supermarket last night and I overheard two young assistants slating some poor cow from the cheese counter who had apparently had *dry* sex with some geek from the bakery; bit of luck it was Jonathon and he'll save his eyesight. I was intrigued not by them but dry sex. Gotta be better than the wet kind. How disappointed to find out it's fumbling with a bit of grinding, fully clothed. That has the same appeal as treating yourself to a cream cake and scraping out the cream. Julie has set me right that the point is, my poor deprived friend, you bump and grind till it's unbearable, tear off the lower clothing and you'll have the best two minutes of sex you've had for a long time. Two minutes? I could manage that; wonder if that includes foreplay, lol.

Friday 23rd November 2014

Girls' night Tina's.

Another engineer arrived and fitted one of the bent hobs, assuring me the defect is so minor I won't notice, at least we'll be functional. Assuring me he will be back Saturday morning with the correct one.

Julie kindly enlightened us this evening to the fact that spot-popping is hers and many others' bag. I thought it was bad enough thinking it's their own zits; nah, it's much better if it's someone else's. Both Tina and Penny were in total agreement with Julie; these are the same people I know that called me disgusting for peeling skin. Er, hello girls. At least what I do doesn't have filth fly out at you, or weeps when I've finished. Skanks. Ooh, gonna razz.

Week 8 since bane of my life began. 'Functional', he said. Yes. Right up till the moment a pan came off the so-called 'minor defect, won't make a difference' hob. The spillage was so bad I've had to rip out the flooring. More money to spend. Then phones to say he can't get here today. Fucking idiot.

Sunday 25th November 2014

Oh my God, found myself tutting earlier.

Was watching as Connor wiped his nose on the sleeve of his coat. I was about to speak when he asks, 'Why are these called cuffs?'

Monday 26th November 2014

Joe football.

Shopping.

Joe asked me why we'd never had the 'sex' talk with our kids? Quite simply, they'd have laughed at us for knowing so little, mate.

Discussed the subject of writing the wills. You know you're getting old when that conversation happens. xx

Mutley vets 10am.

Week 679 of cooker from hell: engineer surfaced this morning with the good news that the new white hob is perfectly straight, goes to fit it and it's broken. Tells me he could replace the part without the guarantee that it would be safe. Mate, last time I listened to him I lost the floor. I aint prepared to blow the back off my house. Threw him out, telling him I'm going back to the store and will be speaking to the manager.

Couldn't wait until Saturday. Cooker saga over, full refund and a handful of vouchers - after they had the audacity to call me a liar, so I told them to poke the cooker up his arse at the same time loudly enlightening all the potential buyers browsing the store as to how shit the products and the service are. Went straight to another store, paid for a new cooker which should be delivered and fitted tomorrow.

Having pushed baldy patch to the back of my mind I thought I'd have a peek and to my amazement it has gone. I confess I did cry.

Unbelievable! Chris has got frostbite! WTF. God only knows how. Stunned the doctor. She might lose her toes; wouldn't mind a look at that, lol. Disappointedly doubt anything that extreme will occur. I'm in shock she has it, more in shock that the doctor has found something actually wrong with her!

Had the new cooker installed today. How sad to be this excited over an appliance? Still, at least now I can cook without fear of saucepans sliding off and killing the cat.

Saturday 1st December 2014

Poker night.

Xmas shopping with Julie.

Bloody hell it's only the 1st and already the shops are filled with the maniac shoppers. I swear Christmas gets here faster every year, and the worst thing is the kids being grown up, when they were little I could spend £500 and they'd have 30 gifts to open now, it's spend £500 and have three measly boxes under the tree. Julie's right: I do worry too much what others are gonna think of me; shallow and superficial, yes. Yes, I've bought many a gift purely for the reason that I'll be judged, paid extreme prices for designer goods not because I wanted to; no, it's because they'll talk about me behind my back. Vented off at Julie, telling her how I'm gonna man up and not do it anymore. She agreed with me that it was shallow and I shouldn't do it, but added that I'm not to include her in this as she likes me buying her expensive gifts. So glad we're spending Christmas at Chloe's; at least this year I won't be the only mug whose cooking for everyone as I can't recall the last time, or indeed ever, that Chris did it.

Up bright and early and it's snowing like a madman outside. I've just texted Julie to get her arse in gear as I'm not resisting the call of the sled. Let's just hope I don't end up in A&E with a blown eardrum again. Must call the others and advise them, just in case I do, that chocolate will suffice, no grapes and definitely no Ribena. The first person that does will be joining me in ICU, bastards. If I'm honest I did question whether I should, but Joe threw down the gauntlet with, 'I know you're having a MLC, you should give thought to your safety, you're not getting any younger.' Game on, mate.

Joe football.

Shopping.

After suffering the crowded supermarket, called Julie to go for a drink. When we got there, propping up the bar were a couple of transvestites, obvious to all but them. Bad wigs, worse make up, forearms like Popeye. Not sure what they were expecting the barman to say when one delusional, mistaking exceptional customer service for flirting, announced, 'I'm flattered, but believe it or not I'm actually a man. 'To which the barman laughed and said, 'No shit, Sherlock. 'Can't repeat what Delores shouted but it weren't very ladylike, lol.

I think the kindest thing to do for Chris is to put her down, bless her. Mum bought her some tablets for relieving blocked sinuses. An hour after taking them she's blown her hooter and has a tissue full of bright yellow liquid. Being Chris she has on some occasion read that the brain is floating in yellow fluid. Took Mum two hours to convince her she wasn't going to die. Clearly wouldn't have been from her head: she aint got no brain to float in it.

Joe came home angrily telling me to expect a letter in the post as he's been caught for curb crawling. He was ranting how it's 'extreme policing', as my jaw hung there in disbelief. He was seconds away from a punch when he said if they'd nicked the guy who had left his van parked illegally, he wouldn't have had to drive on the pavement to get past.

Average day in this family.

Watched a documentary last night on step kids and I gotta say I wouldn't marry a man who had kids from a previous relationship, wouldn't have touched him with a barge pole. Mate, the grief some of these stepparents get is not my bag; ex bitchy partner in the background, no thanks.

Not all are bad, many are amicable, but the ones that are hell: why did they get divorced? They hated each other? Made each other's skin crawl? Bored the shit out of you, bullied you, made you feel like crap, held you back in life? Whatever the reason, it usually ends up a battlefield with endless shouting and fighting that pushes for the Decree Absolute. Whether the reason is large or small it's good enough to separate. So why do so many divorced couples keep up the fight long after the divorce? Might as well have stayed unhappily married, saved your money. What is the point? You wanted out, so stay out, but no, you will bitch and create hell at every opportunity, dragging yourself, the family and, most alarmingly, the kids through more crap. Anyone who's been through a divorce knows how hard it can be; the wounds stay open for quite a while. But seriously, I know couples who still don't behave civilly after ten years apart. All the technical stuff gets sorted by the courts - money, possessions, property and access to the children - so there's no excuse.

Thursday 6th December 2014

Elizabeth has arrived at her sister's and Chloe has gone to her mum's. Looking forward to Friday's girls' night here.

I'm in favour of technology but I do think it has spoilt so much for kids:MP3s, mobile phones, computers... great fun, but encourages loneliness. Gone are the days of standing in line for the latest hit record released by your favourite heartthrob. Once purchased you'd be rushing home, knocking on friends' doors on the way. By the time I'd get back to mine there would be a dozen of us tearing up the stairs, piling onto the bed. They would wait with bated breath as I would open the record player and carefully place the needle onto the record. A silence would be maintained for the first playing, then a group discussion would prevail consisting mainly of 'Oh, oooh, he's the greatest, how cool', and the 'I'm gonna marry him!' Within an hour every person present would not only know the lyrics by heart, but we'd have a dance routine to accompany it. The debates for and against said artist would continue all day.

Socially it did wonders for us kids: there were no hostilities when we piled outside in the street where we would teach anyone the routine, which seemed so much more impressive when there was 30 of us synchronized, much to the oldies dismay. OK, talking about pop stars or fashion wasn't rocket science but it got us communicating, gave us something in common, a reason to be nice to each other. Whereas today's music gadgets may hold more tunes than we ever owned, but where's the fun and interaction?

Mmm, Donny Osmond… would have back then, and would definitely now.

Saturday 8th December 2014

Been out burning up Joe's credit card. The three of us had decided to go up west and make the most of the time. Chloe and Elizabeth have headed off so I'm going to cook me and Joe a nice meal and crack open a nice bottle of wine (shocker).Having spent the last 48 hours in the company of females it made me stop and think how shitty I can be to Joe. Poor bloke deserves better.

Sunday 9th December 2014

I'd texted Joe telling him dinner would be ready by seven. He strolls in -oh, I'm sorry, *crawls* through the door at nine, still holding the half-eaten kebab, attempting to apologise for being late. Has five attempts at telling me he loves me. I was in a forgiving mood, all was good, then he declares that he never knew what happiness was until he married me, but by then it was too late. How he feels the years we've spent together has been an adventure, a bit like going off to war, a war where in fact you sleep with the enemy. Then it seemed he was on a roll, with no stone unturned it ended with him saying marriage is about being committed. So does being fucking mental, mate.

Tuesday 11th December 2014

Joe spent yesterday trying to convince me that he had no recollection of Sunday's outburst, even desperately trying the 'Someone must have slipped me a Mickey. 'At least when I'm horrible I'm upfront about it. Too be honest I can't be asked to argue about it anymore; these days I look forward to a dull evening in.

Wednesday 12th December 2014

Hairdresser 5pm.
　　Is there a conspiracy against me? Julie called me this morning at half nine and says 'Sorry, did I wake you up?'I aint that old, although I have noticed more often that I ache from top to toe, and what don't ache don't work,

Sam, Connor, Daisy Xmas play 3pm

Sam was Joseph, Daisy an angel, and Connor- a jellyfish? Nope, I didn't get it. From the moment they got on the stage I beamed with pride, struggled not to cry as they waved, smiled as Daisy blew me a kiss, whilst looking about daring one person to laugh as they fluffed their lines. Raising kids is 90% hardship, misery and tears, but the 10% good far outweighs the bad.

Video and DVD players are a cool invention, yet are another form of technology that has deprived kids in some way: where's the excitement when the kids put a film on? How different for us, when we'd hear the Warner Brothers tune? How early would we get up So's not to miss the *Banana Splits*, how gutted we'd feel if we found a film on telly halfway through, knowing that it wouldn't be repeated for years if ever. It's not that we necessarily appreciated stuff more, it was more that we didn't take for granted it would be there.

Saturday 15th December 2014

Arthur's 46th birthday.

Leg wax 2pm.

How come you never notice a potato has gone rotten until your finger slips into the underside, releasing a squelch and a stench that could gag a Billy goat?

George's 28th birthday.

Jackie said that George had received all his gifts from us in time for his birthday. She's missing him terribly, but I guess that's the downside of being a soldier's wife. Other than power cuts, all else is good on camp. Ya see, power cuts: there's another rarity now that was common in our childhood. Shame, really, cos I liked them: our lives didn't come to a standstill, we made shadows with our hands, searching for the candles that parents always kept for such occasions but could never remember where the safe place was, lol. But mostly a lack of power to a house caused people to talk. I think the people in charge of the national grid now should just throw the switch sometimes for the hell of it, and restore some much-needed communication.

Thursday 20th December 2014

Sam asked me what game computer did I have when I was little; looked dumbstruck when I said they hadn't been invented. He laughed and asked, 'How did you live, Nan?' Cheers, buddy. To be honest, I'm glad we didn't. I also think as parents we need to monitor and restrict the time kids spend playing them: far too many will sit playing a game when they should be outside playing. It's far too easy for youngsters to withdraw into their own company.

I can't argue that mobile phones and PCs open the doors for many housebound people: they can shop, buy, discover all sorts online; allows them to communicate via email or chat live on the social networks, keeping in touch with family and friends.

Then of course there's the bad side, which is it attracts perverts and its brother. Better learn to decipher code as kids all write in it, that's if you even get to read it before they shut the window down. Youngsters are happy to write incoherent shit for hours but don't know how to hold a conversation face to face for five minutes. And technology is seen as progress.

Friday 21st December 2014

The technology debate rages on and climaxes with toys: what can we buy a child that requires imagination? Where's all the simple Lego, the Meccano, the simple doll's house? How many games did we play that involved one tennis ball? Off-Ground Touch, He Ball, Sting Ball, Bulldog, Run Outs, Weasel, Tin Tan Tonny, Curbsie, Hopscotch, Scoobydoo, Polo, Kiss Chase, Knock Down Ginger…the list is endless. Call 'Vaynites' when someone needed a time out: honourable.Yeah, we sometimes fell out with each other; within a day it was forgotten, not like now where everything's a grudge that ends in violence. It's up to the parents to guide the kids; mine have all spent summers playing ball games, chalking, water-bombing (every kid learns quickly that the expensive enormous water gun is no match for the lightweight washing-up liquid bottle), grass fights, puddle-hopping… all good clean fun. I'm as guilty as the rest for spending hundreds of pounds on the latest must-haves, yet it's the other stuff they remember most.

We're all off to Scotland tomorrow to spend Christmas at the farm.

Saturday 22nd December 2014

All of us have arrived here in Scotland. The live turkey keeps following Connor; he is not happy.

Elizabeth bought his and hers chamois leather-lined wellies, $442 dollars worth, and dressed them both head to toe in Chanel.

Joe's sporting a goatee looks like he's swallowed a squirrel. Julie, beside herself, stated she'd give anything to rescue said squirrel right now. Freak. Gonna have to sleep with one eye open with her under the same roof as Joe.

Us females are heading into the city tonight. Bit of luck, Julie will exhaust herself on the local cuisine.

Sunday 23rd December 2014

JJ's nightclub: excellent venue, excellent music and the cheesiest pick-up lines I've ever heard. 'D'ya have a library card cuz ad like ta check ye out', 'Is there a mirror in ya drawers? Cuz I can see masel in em. lol.

Jaki and Jeni, having been led to believe their parents were divorcing (Pauls ruse to ensure they'd come home for Christmas), had decided to save some news of their own until they got here. Both arrived at the farm with a husband each (twin bros) and both the girls are pregnant with twins. Chloe shrieked and burst into tears, Joe had to restrain Paul, lol. All ended well, the girls are moving back to the farm for good to raise the babies, four grandchildren in one hit. Cool. Turning point for Paul was the news that his new sons-in-law are absolutely minted.

Breakthrough on Connor's phobia of fowl: the turkey hasn't left his side and now Connor calls him Terrance aka Butterball, so it seems shickens is OK now.

There is always a downside to the cure of a phobia; Paul and Joe had to go searching the city to buy a shop-sold turkey late afternoon yesterday, as Chloe didn't have the heart to kill Terrance.

The evening brought the locals for a drink. Derek asked me what it would take to get a kiss under the mistletoe. He didn't look impressed when I said 'Nothing short of anaesthetic, mate. 'I made sure all mistletoe was gone before drinking any 'in jar with no name'.

Two hours into the fun and two sheets to the wind, Chloe was washing the turkey, trips, shoots the bird across the floor with skills that only a curling champion could have matched.

Dutifully we took turns to take the farm feline outside for a wee as poor alley cat don't go out no more alone, after he was attacked by a pair of robins. He had to have five stitches in his head and is now frightened of his own shadow and won't go out without an escort. Nice to see that everything in our lives is mental.

This morning began with the exciting frenzied opening of presents: Joe, not the kids, lol. Chloe heaved every time she opened the oven door. Virgil, having spotted alley cat skulking off with the discarded raw turkey neck and giblets, reaches behind the sofa and takes it from the pilfering coward. Connor, having seen this, screams 'Virgil's got a really big willy!'All heads shot in his direction. Abigail smiled and Julie's eyes lit up. Really, girls?

We made it to dinner time like any other normal family. Well, that's if you ignore the turkey sitting up at the table with a plate of corn. Dinner was great and the homemade Christmas pudding looked amazing. Paul lit the brandy-coated cake, the flame engulfed everything in a 2 foot radius including Terrence's tail feathers. With a squawk he legs it out across the yard and ignites the haystack. It's now five o'clock, all fires are out, the kids are playing quietly and apart from me and Jackie, everybody else it seems is napping.

Merry Christmas. xx

Wednesday 26th December 2014

Boxing Day.

You couldn't write the script for us! Around seven last night Jackie went into labour. We all ran about in a panic, called an ambulance, only to be told 'It will take a while to get there', and not to panic. Oh lol! Jackie's body didn't want to wait, and with the contractions coming only minutes apart we were having a united breakdown. Then amid the madness Chris and Virgil calmly began ordering us to fetch and carry clean sheets, towels, warm water. We watched gobsmacked as the usually hysterical Chris, aided by Virgil, delivered her grandchild. Dillon weighed in at 8 pounds 3 ounces. Baby's perfect, Jackie's fine.

And my sister is a legend. xx

Saturday 29th December 2014

Friday was Leigh's sixteenth birthday. We said we'd take her to the city, but she chose to stay in and fuss over Dillon. Can't say I blame her, we all have trouble putting him down.

Andy and Jess headed off to Jessica's parents in the morning, and Penny and Mark arrived here after dropping Rhianne and Charlie off at their Nan's.

As its Tony's birthday today the men are taking him shooting. We're expecting George to arrive sometime after twelve as he's been granted special leave to come and see his son. Tina and Terry should be arriving from Aspen this evening for New Year. Other than that, all's good.

Monday 31st December 2014

Barn Dance at the village hall.

Well, I've reached the end of another year, older and wiser. Well, older anyway. We have a new addition to the family – well two, if you count Terrance aka Butterball; Chris has managed not to die; Daisy learned a new word, even if it was 'dickhead'. I've seen hair go and come; I lived to see Julie be less promiscuous than Elizabeth; seen my best friend move a million miles away; and as for the mid-life crisis... we're all getting old, we all have bits that don't look the same or indeed function the same, so what if Joe's aggravating habits are really aggravating me? Does it really matter that I feel like a teenager trapped in an old person's body? This is life, this is my life. Now, where's that skimpy dress from Morton's? There is a jar of something out there with my name on it. Happy New Year.